White Tulips

By

Cheryl A. Daniels

READING ENTERTAINMENT
FOR THE ENTIRE FAMILY

Copyright© December 2013 Cheryl A. Daniels

Cover Art: Dawne Dominque Copyright December 2012

Editor: Kase J. Reed

Line Editor: Chynna Laird

Genre: Topaz Light Christian Romance Novella

Word Count: 25,858

ISBN: TPEB000000031

ISBN-13: 978-0615937274 Topaz Publishing

ISBN-10:0615937276

Topaz Publishing, LLC

USA

www.topazpublishingllc.com

Topaz Publishing, LLC

Available in E-Book, and E-Book CD

Thank you for buying a product of Topaz Publishing

Quality Reading for the Entire Family

DEDICATION

I dedicate this book to my parents, Jethan and Rosie Lee, for instilling a profound love and respect for God in me.

White Tulips

The Flower of Forgiveness

After a terrible car wreck, Cassidy Fallow's family secrets are revealed. She finds out that her mother had an affair, and now questions the man she believes is her father.

Her mother was inebriated the night of the accident, and drove the SUV recklessly. As a result, she lost her life. Once, Cassidy was a blossoming artist—a socialite with exhibits demanding her attention. Now, consumed with grief, her previous life doesn't matter and she withdraws from society. To make matters worse, Cassidy has fallen for the Christian detective her family has wronged. Who is God anyway, and why does this handsome man think she needs him? Interracial Romance BW/WM, Christian, Inspirational & Sweet Romance. Cheryl A. Daniels, Topazpublishingllc.com http://CherylADaniels.com

CONTENTS

ACKNOWLEDGMENTS

To my husband Keith, my children: Tiphanni, Donald, Kindrik, and Meaghan. Thank you for believing in me and my work. I love and appreciate you all.

To my siblings: James, Warren, and Valencia. Thank you for allowing me, the baby of the bunch, to tag along. Each of you have contributed to my imagination in different, but equally important ways.

To Max and the rest of my family at Topaz Publishing. Words cannot express the depth of my gratitude for your guidance and patience. My dream wouldn't have become a reality if not for your faith in my writing ability.

Many people have impacted my life and deserve recognition. However, I can't name you all. Please know that I hold each of you in my heart, and you're not forgotten.

Cheryl

Cheryl A. Daniels, Author

Topaz Publishing, llc.com

White Tulips

The Flower of Forgiveness

CHAPTER ONE

The black SUV sped along the icy, wet Wyoming road. A frigid wind sporadically pushed the vehicle into the other lane. Even with all-weather tires, the SUV continued to skid across the asphalt in some places. Small ice pellets fell to the ground — another thief of nature, stealing the driver's view.

Sleet pounded heavily against the vehicle causing it to hydroplane. Cassidy bit her fingernails. Her body jerked forward, and her heart pounded as if seeking refuge outside her anxiety-ridden body. She watched her mother adjust the speed and straighten the steering wheel, only to have the vehicle hydroplane again. SUV and driver tangoed intermittently, each wanting to take the lead.

Dangers of the poorly lit, ice-glazed road didn't seem to faze Karen and Charles, Cassidy's parents. Their argument escalated with every gust of wind. Neither the flickering windshield wipers, nor the icy pellets pounding the SUV, could mask the shouting inside the automobile. Periodically her mother would cry, adding fuel to an already explosive situation.

As a child, Cassidy disliked when her parents argued. Their altercations made her feel insecure and guilty. Now, at age twenty-five, their bickering was still abhorrent and exhausting. Her mother became so consumed with arguing that nothing else mattered, including the current dangerous conditions of the road.

Though worried her fear would only intensify the situation, Cassidy spoke out. "Mom, would you like for me to drive?" Already too scared to concentrate, she tried desperately to dampen the anxiety in her voice.

Her mother glared at her through the rearview mirror, and then she narrowed her eyes. "No Cassie," she scolded. "I don't need you to drive. I'm just fine, alright?"

Under her mother's curt words, Cassidy blinked, looking apologetically. "Mom, I only made that suggestion because my eyesight is better than yours, especially at night."

Charles turned to face his wife. "I agree, Karen. You should let one of us drive. Pull over."

"I said I'm fine!" Once again, Karen looked into the rear view mirror and frowned, as if warning Cassidy to let it go.

Cassidy gave her attention to the flowers next to her, hoping to take her mind off her parents. Though white tulips graced their house, red roses were always her favorite. Her father had given them to her for having another successful art exhibit. She'd sold almost all of her paintings. Touching the delicate petals, Cassidy beamed with pride, never dreaming her career would be so successful and lucrative.

A few of the flowers shifted as the SUV hydroplaned again, bringing Cassidy back into focus. Her mother still waged war on her father, and the sight sickened her.

Karen turned her head from the road to look at Charles. "Just admit it, Charles. I saw you flirting! Why do you always flirt in front of me? And this time, at Cassie's art exhibit!"

Charles snorted, then answered, "I'm sixty years old, Karen—too old to flirt with a woman half my age. It would be inappropriate and disrespectful to behave in such a manner — particularly in front of my daughter."

Sitting in the middle of the back seat, Cassidy could see the side of her mother's face, which was illuminated by the incandescent light of the dashboard. She thought she saw her mother's nostrils flare as she slammed her fist against the steering wheel. "I'm your wife, Charles. Respect me!"

Cassidy sighed. *"Good grief!"* Her parents had been having the same argument for most of her life. Grade school through grad school, delusional or not, her mother always accused her father of infidelity.

Both parents were attractive for any age. Women often flirted with her dad. His bedroom eyes had a come-hither appearance, and boy did women come hither. His curly, low cut hair had only a hint of gray, and Charles's toned physique would rival any thirty-year-old male.

Her mother didn't work out as much as her father, so her body was soft, not muscled. She had aged gracefully, and although thin in stature, she was still feminine. Whatever conviction she lacked in exercising, she more than made up for through her beauty regimen. Facials, lotions, creams, scrubs, you name it. Between expensive products and her aesthetician, Karen's honey colored skin remained unblemished and smooth. Her face was delicate, yet strong, and her cheekbones remained high. With the help of an expensive hairdresser, Karen's fiery reddish-brown hair accentuated her piercing hazel eyes.

People spoke of how much Cassidy resembled her mother. When she looked in the mirror, sometimes she'd see her mother staring back. With the exception of auburn hair, her chocolate-colored eyes, and other features were solely hers, including her skin tone. Cassidy's skin was more café au lait, with a lot of au lait.

Continuing to swear obscenities at her father, her mother berated herself for being a fool for so long. "This marriage is over!"

Cassidy folded her arms. *"Ten more minutes and we'll be home."* Relief washed over her for a brief moment.

The vehicle swerved on the winding two-lane road. Cassidy's heart leaped in her chest, and a shiver ran down her spine. "Mom, please pull over." She held back the scream building inside. "I think you've had too much to drink." There. She'd finally said what she'd been thinking. Her mother was intoxicated and shouldn't be driving.

Her mother raised her eyes. Inside the rearview mirror, a look of betrayal was etched on her face. Right then Cassidy had no desire to pacify her. They swerved into the wrong lane once again, throwing Cassidy against the window. Glaring headlights rushed toward them, blinding her. She widened her eyes, and her heart raced.

"Karen!" Charles tried to wrestle the steering wheel from her grasp.

As the lights flooded the vehicle, Karen screamed. Quickly, she hit the brakes, but the SUV didn't stop. It skidded across the road, then slammed into the oncoming vehicle.

Shattering glass and thunderous sounds of metal against metal were deafening. The SUV flipped over, and landed upside down. Sleet pelted Cassidy's warm face. Her eyes burned and watered. Gas fumes, smoke and burnt rubber fouled the air. Chemicals from the air bag, added to the pungent mixture.

When Cassidy tried to move, the seat belt cut deep into her shoulder. Inside her mouth, was the taste of blood and rose petals. Excruciating pain ravaged her body.

"Mom, Dad?" Cassidy wasn't sure if the words actually left her lips. Neither parent responded.

"I think they're all dead." She heard a voice say. Immediately, she lost consciousness

CHAPTER TWO

Three weeks after the accident, Cassidy stood before the bay window. The Japanese garden was supposed to inspire serenity. Unfortunately, the frozen expensive shrubbery fell short of its promise.

Her mother loved Asian culture. She felt their beliefs were inspiring as they still held the same values as they had several millennia ago. A few years earlier, her mother even had their house Feng Shui. Any given room had reds, pinks, greens, blues, and yellows. Every room had something white inside. Most times, the white décor came from the beauty of white tulips. Tulips were the only flowers her mother ever bought.

These days, the white was missing inside their home. When her mother died, the white blossoms soon withered away. Neither she nor her father had bothered to replace them. Without the calming effect of the white flowers, and the warmth of her mother's spirit, the spacious home appeared cold. A warm fireplace couldn't nullify the coldness of despair.

At that moment, Cassidy was supposed to be painting. Instead, inspiration evaded her. What a pity. Painting was the one thing that had never let her down. After placing her paintbrush in a turpentine-filled jar, she sighed. The only thing that truly gave her solace had died with her mother. Happiness was a thing of the past. She wanted to paint, but she also needed her mother. As sad as things appeared, Cassidy knew she'd never have either again.

Fatigued by sorrow and sleep deprivation, she yawned. Anger infested her body. She wiped a tear from her eye, staining her cheek with red paint. She grieved one parent, while coping with her anger at the other. Was she angry with her father for arguing with her mother that night? Or, was it because her mother's accusation had some merit? There was no way to be sure. After all, she had also seen him flirting with women.

With the door to her studio open, Cassidy heard her father's footsteps as he walked into the living room. When the sound of his feet moving stopped, she turned to see him hovering by the studio door. Suddenly, the doorbell rang. Charles gave her a puzzled expression. Since the funeral, neither had contact with the outside world.

Curious to see who was at the door, Cassidy grasped a paint-stained rag from the table where jars of paint and brushes were neatly arranged. Once she wiped her hands, she brushed strands of unkempt hair behind her ears.

After closing her makeshift studio door, Cassidy went into the foyer. Her mother made sure their home was always spotless, at least Mrs. Hazel, their housekeeper, did. Much like the rest of the house, the marbled floors were dusty. Cassidy sighed with disappointment, then made a mental note to call Mrs. Hazel in the morning.

Through the window, she saw that their shrubbery was frozen with ice. Consumed by grief, neither of them made any attempt to protect the plants from the cold. Charles opened the front door. A man was standing on the porch. He was dressed in jeans, a red sweater, and a black leather coat. He handed

Charles some mail.

"Good afternoon, sir. Your mailman must've thought I lived here. He gave me your mail as I walked up."

Charles reached for the mail, and frowned. "May I help you?"

"My name is Liam Papadakis." He presented a detective's shield. "This is just for identification purposes, sir. I'm not here under official capacity. This is personal."

Charles closed the door halfway. "I don't care what your badge says. What do you want?" Undisguised rudeness was in his voice.

He gave Cassidy the mail then ushered her behind him. She peeked over her father's shoulder. His name was familiar to her. Liam Papadakis was the other person involved in the accident.

Her father stood six one, and Liam was a few inches taller him. In his coat, Cassidy could see that his body was muscular. He appeared to be in his early thirties, with a surfer boy's good looks. Blue-gray eyes and wavy black hair completed the picture. On his chin there was a small healing scar. However, the blemish didn't diminish his good looks. If anything, the flaw added something more.

After a few seconds, Liam's lips formed a taut smile. He pointed at Cassidy's face. "You have a little something beneath your eye."

Cassidy wiped her face with her forearm. "Thank you." She wasn't sure if his smile was genuine, or if his smirk had broken her trance. Her cheeks felt flushed, realizing she'd been staring. "How can we help you?" She caressed her father's waist. "Dad, let him in."

As if confused by her invitation, her father stared at her. Other than wanting to know more about him, she wasn't clear about her true motives.

Her father continued to block the door. Apparently, he didn't feel the same way. "You have all of our insurance information. And the last I heard, you've already been compensated. So you need to either talk to our insurance company, or our attorney."

Liam pointed to a new black truck sitting in front of their house. "Sir, that's my new, fully loaded truck. I'm truly blessed to be alive. Any bruises and scratches I have will heal. I'm not going to sue you. If that's what you think, you can relax."

From Cassidy's experience, her father trusted no one, so the man was talking in vain.

She knew he would no sooner let this man through the door than he would Charles Manson. Curious herself as to why the visit was necessary, she tugged on her father's flexed arm. "Dad," she said firmly. "Let him in."

With a stony expression, he stepped back, and stumbled over the rug.

Liam wiped his feet on the doormat, and crossed the threshold. He held Charles' gaze. "Thank you."

Liam's movements were fluid, almost hypnotizing. Cassidy couldn't take her eyes off him. If his surname didn't give away his Greek heritage, his beautiful olive skin did. She couldn't help but admire his striking appearance.

Charles frowned at Liam, his stare imposing. "What do you want?"

Liam recoiled, and Cassidy noticed the venom in her father's voice. "I've been meaning to give this back to you." He pulled a gold locket from his pocket.

A few seconds passed before Charles spoke. "Where did you get that?"

"The hospital, or the police, put this locket

with my personal belongings. Inside, the inscription inside says, *To KF with love.* I assumed KF stood for Karen Fallows."

Hearing the story, Cassidy's eyes glistened. "That's Mom's necklace!" She opened her palm, and Liam placed the necklace in her hand. "We've been looking for this." Fighting her grief, she managed a smile. "Thank you, Mr. Papadakis."

"Don't thank me just yet." He took a step backwards. "I wanted to return the necklace. In addition, I also wanted to meet the kind of people who would let a drunken person get behind the wheel of a car."

Taken aback by his statement, and his spiteful tone, Cassidy winced. "W-what?" There was truth in his words. Someone outside their family knew their dirty little secret.

Charles stiffened, his eyes flashed, then he pulled Cassidy behind him again. "Get the hell out of my house! We're not drunks. Karen made a mistake. She paid for that mistake with her life!"

Leaving the men to sort out their differences Cassidy backed away from the door. Their conversation wasn't one she wanted to participate in. She opened the clasp on the necklace and secured her mother's pendent around her neck. Her father had placed the mail on the end table, and she picked it up. As she shuffled through the mail, one of the envelopes drew her attention. The letter came from the mobile blood bank at St. Francis Hospital. After opening the letter, she read it, then said softly, "This can't be right."

Seemingly, the panicked tone of her voice stopped the men from arguing. Her father's gaze met hers. "What's wrong?"

She gave the letter to him. "They want me to donate plasma, because my blood type is AB. They want you to donate blood, because your blood type is O. There's been some mistake. You're my father. Type O doesn't produce type AB."

Charles reached for the letter. He folded it, then shoved it back inside the envelope. "We'll discuss this later." Hard lines were visual on his face. He turned to Liam. "Is there anything else you wanted? If not, goodbye."

Cassidy positioned herself between the two men. Up close, she could see the dark circles and bags under her father's eyes. Sleep must've evaded him as it had her. "We'll discuss what later, Dad?"

Her father glanced at her uneasily, and let out an exasperated sigh. "Not now, Cass. Let me get rid of Mr. Papadakis, then give me a few minutes to think."

The serious tone of his voice warned her that he was hiding something painful. She bit her lip. "What's there to think about? Obviously, the letter is wrong. Isn't it, Daddy?" He didn't reply. She saw fear growing in her father's eyes. "Dad?"

Charles turned his face from her view. A muscle jumped in his neck. "Cassidy, please. Not now." Not giving Liam a subtle hint, he swung the door wide opened.

Liam turned toward the door. "I guess that means my time is up. I'll leave."

Charles clenched his teeth. "You should've never come here in the first place."

Liam walked out the door without saying another word. Standing on the front porch, he didn't bother to close the front door.

Immediately, Charles slammed the door, then averted his eyes from Cassidy. He placed the letter on the sofa table, walked to the bar, then grabbed a soda from the fridge.

Her father's actions were remote. Cassidy watched him and frowned. She threw the rest of the mail in a pile atop the peculiar letter, and then she followed closely on his heels. "Daddy. You always call me Cass. A moment ago, you called me Cassidy. You only call my full name when something is seriously wrong. Dad, please tell me this letter is wrong."

There was a moment of silence. He raked his fingers through his hair, then rubbed his chin. "Let's not do this right now, please." His eyes flitted around the room in every direction except hers.

Hearing his words, Cassidy's heart pounded. *"Why won't he just deny the letter?"* She stood toe to toe with him. Of everyone she knew, his face was the most familiar to her, yet at that exact moment he looked foreign. "Dad, I need to hear you say this letter is wrong, and I need to hear you say it right now."

Her father sighed, and muttered something under his breath. He opened his mouth as if to reply, instead he trailed off. Several times he reached out for her, only to stop midway. "No, the letter isn't wrong. I'm not your biological father."

Cassidy widened her eyes. She held back the scream inside her throat. "What?" Her heartbeat pounded wildly as her legs gave out.

However, before she fell, she leaned against the bar. "Why would my parents keep this secret from me?"

His voice was barely above a whisper. "The secret wasn't mine to tell." If he tried to sound composed, he failed. She heard a faint tremor in his voice.

Cassidy felt betrayed by the people she trusted most. For the second time in her life, she was furious with her father. "Who's my father?" She gazed at him with outrage, daring him not to answer her question.

With his face torn in anguish, her father turned. "I'm your father! When you were sick, I stayed up with you. Every scrapped knee, I bandaged. Every tennis match, every dance recital and every graduation, I was there. I don't care what our DNA says, you're my daughter."

Unable to contain herself, Cassidy sobbed. "You and mom were married for years before I was born. Was I adopted?" She grasped a hand full of reddish brown hair, and shook her head. "No, I look too much like Mom. How is it possible that you aren't my father?"

Charles drank his soda, and didn't answer.

"Answer me, Dad!" She pounded her fist

against the bar.

Suddenly, Charles blasted. "Karen had an affair, all right?" He loosened the collar on his shirt. "Is that what you wanted to hear? Your mother cheated on me, okay? Funny. She always called me out for doing what she'd done our entire marriage." Under the strain of his voice, the veins in his neck pulsated.

Cassidy slumped against the bar in an effort to catch her breath. "I don't believe you! Who would Mom have an affair with? The only men I ever saw her with, were you and Uncle Peter."

Her father's customary self-control unraveled. "We will talk about this later."

"Who did Mom have an affair with?" she pressed. Never before had she raised her voice to either parent. She thought having them as parents was a blessing. Except for the bickering, she believed their parenting skills were impeccable.

With his face contorted into a frown, Charles jerked in reaction to the anomaly. He opened his mouth to speak, but nothing came out. Only one person could have pained his face so gravely.

From somewhere deep within, a suddenly

obvious reality settled inside her. Cassidy's anxiety ridden body slumped down further, and her sweaty palms held on tighter to the bar. "It's Peter Hass, isn't it?"

Her father stiffened. He didn't have to answer at that point. Really, she wasn't sure if she wanted him to. On second thought, she had to know. The only thing that could be worse than knowing would be to not know. She hoped her eyes pleaded with him enough to convince him to answer.

He slightly nodded once. "I believe so." His eyes darkened. Cassidy could see him holding tears at bay.

As a child, Peter always took an interest in her, insisting she call him Uncle Peter. He was present at every major event in her life. And like a broken record, he repeatedly commented about how their eyes and skin tones were the same. She crossed her arms over her chest. Her gaze was fixed on Charles. "How long have you known, Dad?"

Charles exhaled. That time, he picked up a glass and poured himself a shot of whiskey. "When you were ten, a doctor told me I'd been sterile my whole life." He tried to touch

Cassidy's shoulder, but she flinched. Though she saw the pain in his eyes, she was too hurt to care.

"Cass, I loved Karen. And I love you. Peter had been my best friend since grade school. I asked him to look after my wife whenever I was out of town. As you know, that was most of the time. I worked such long hours, that I practically threw Karen into his arms. I started cheating when I stopped going out of town. That's when I saw them together. I never told her, I knew." As if exhausted, he sighed. "Does it matter? Have I ever *not* been your father?"

Cassidy's car keys were on the sofa table. She reached for them. "I'm leaving."

"Where are you going?" The deep angry tone to her dad's voice had all but disappeared.

"Out!" She threw on her coat, wrapped a scarf around her neck, and darted out the door.

CHAPTER THREE

*W*hen Cassidy ran out of the house, she had no idea where she was going. She only knew she had to leave. The intensity of the argument had risen higher than any argument they'd ever had. Cassidy wasn't prepared to hear her father tell her that her whole life had been a lie. Nor was she prepared to learn he wasn't her father. Using the sleeve of her coat, she wiped tears from her eyes. Could she take another blow of reality without completely surrendering to grief? How could one person simultaneously endure so much pain and agony?

She pulled her car into the driveway of Bailey's Grill & Pub. The parking lot was full. She found a parking space on the side of the street. Bailey's was known for its burgers and fries. While her stomach growled, her mind raced with questions only a mother could answer. Since Karen was dead, the questions were futile. The solemn thought made her body tense. Hoping the stress was nothing a good burger couldn't fix, she hopped out of the car.

Once inside, the ten-minute wait the hostess had promised, turned into thirty. It took even longer for her dinner to arrive. On a whim, she decided to try the blueberry martinis. Since she wasn't a drinker, Cassidy hoped the strong drinks would help her relax. After eating, she paid her bill, then got up to leave. After zigzagging through the maze of people she finally reached the exit door.

"Thank you for coming to Bailey's. Be careful driving home," she heard the hostess say to the customer in front of her.

The man pulled on his gloves. "Thank you. Once again, the food was great."

His voice was familiar. Cassidy froze. Not three hours earlier, that same voice was in her house. She watched Liam as he walked out the door.

Right on cue, the hostess smiled at her just as she reached the station. "Goodnight ma'am. Thank you for coming to Bailey's."

Cassidy wondered if she gave the same spiel to everyone as they left. Outside, she saw

Liam stoop to pick up his fallen scarf. Before she could get out of his sight, she turned around and puked into a nearby bush. She worried that her constant retching had caught his attention. For a split second, she contemplated running, except she couldn't move. She'd had enough of Liam. More than she'd bargained for. After all, he was the catalyst for horrible events in her life. First, there was the car accident and then he brought the piece of paper that further altered her life.

Still on her knees, Cassidy sighed.

Liam strolled over to her. "Cassidy?" Even though she saw him approaching, she jumped when he said her name. Liam backed out of her personal space, and touched his chest. "It's me. Liam Papadakis. We met at your house this evening."

With eyes watering, Cassidy looked at his shoes, then wiped her mouth with the back of her hand. Next, she noticed his jeans, and lastly his concerned face. "Dear Lord," she muttered, "why me?" She felt her face get hot. Saliva formed at the side of her mouth. Absently, she tugged at what should've been her coat. Where was her coat? She couldn't remember. She'd walked out of Baily's, sans her coat. Having no other choice, she used the hem of her shirt to wipe her mouth. "What are you doing here?"

"I stopped here for dinner." His eyes softened, and he lowered his hand to help her up. "Are you okay?"

Cassidy slapped his hand. "Yes. Now go away." Quickly, she whirled around, and threw up again. This time, she finished with dry heaves.

Liam brush tangled hair from her face and then pulled it into a ponytail. His hands felt wonderful stroking her locks from her face. After a few moments of stroking Cassidy's hair, he allowed her hair to fall into her face. He shifted his weight as if embarrassed by the unexpected intimacy they'd shared. Hastily, he shoved his hands inside the pockets of his jeans. Cassidy placed a handful of hair over her nose, wondering if an odor from her strands had caused his reaction. That morning she used Jasmine shampoo, the scent was still pronounced. *"What's his problem?"*

After taking a handkerchief out of his coat pocket, Liam kneeled and then gave it to her. He stood up again. "You're not driving. Are you?"

Cassidy furrowed her brows. Her eyes

blazed. Remembering his earlier accusation that they were all drunks, she became annoyed. "I'm not going to drive intoxicated, if that's what you're asking. The bartender called me a cab. I'm waiting out here because it's hot in there."

As if taking in their surroundings, she followed Liam's eyes as he cast his gaze about the area. The plants were frozen, as were the trees, and foliage on the icy ground. Steam rolled from their lips and snowflakes had begun to fall. He took off his leather coat and placed it around Cassidy's shoulders. Immediately, he drew in a breath with a shiver. She felt guilty. His body obviously missed the protection the coat gave.

Liam held out his hand to assist her to her feet. "It's cold out here. Come on, I'll take you home."

Staring into Liam's sympathetic eyes, Cassidy wrapped herself inside the warmth of the coat. "Why are you being so nice to me?"

He shrugged. "I'm a nice guy. Putting his arm around her waist, he assisted her until she found her footing. "Is your coat still inside the pub?"

She glanced up at him quizzically. "What?"

"Your coat." Liam braced her against his hip. "Did you forget your coat inside Bailey's?"

Cassidy scratched her temple. "I guess so." Her mind searched for the answer. "Can you please just take me home?"

Liam grimaced. "I said I would." He ran his fingers through his hair. "I'm trying here, okay? Just give me a minute," he replied harshly. The wind blew her hair into his face. He took a deep breath. "Your hair smells like jasmine."

"Thanks. My mother bought…." Cassidy's eyes watered, and her teeth chattered. "I really want to go home."

After helping her into his truck, Liam clasped the seatbelt across her body, closed the door, then jogged to the driver's side.

CHAPTER FOUR

*T*he road was completely dark. The drive reminded Cassidy of the night of the accident. Snowflakes melted as soon as they touched the ground, making the roads slippery, just like that night. Headlights coming from

head. Her father's words were cruel and intimidating. Did Liam regret bringing nowhere, threaten to pull her deeper into despair. Reeling with fear, she wrapped Liam's coat tightly around her.

As the car parked into the driveway, the porch light came on. *"You should've never come here in the first place."* Those words echoed inside her her home? She heard him inhale deeply, then exhale. He probably wanted to speed away. Any sane person would. However a sane person would've pretended not to see her sprawled on the sidewalk.

Liam got out of his truck then opened the passenger door. "I'll carry you inside."

"I can walk, Liam." Cassidy stumbled out of the car, yet had to sit back down.

"Like I said, I'll carry you." He picked her up, then carried her to the door, almost dropping her when he pressed the doorbell.

Charles opened the door right away with a scowl intact. "Cassidy!" He took her out of Liam's arms. She heard the front door close. "What's wrong with her?"

"I found her throwing up on the sidewalk, without her coat." There's nothing wrong with her. She's just drunk." The closeness of Liam's voice told her that he also came inside their house.

Her eyes were barely open, yet and still she saw Charles reprimand Liam with his eyes. She'd seen that facial expression countless times.

Liam swallowed, and took a step backwards. "At least, I think she's drunk," he added, like an afterthought.

Being a dominating person, her father could have unnerving effects on people. His stare could bring the hardest man to his knees.

"Cassidy hardly ever drinks, and she

certainly doesn't get inebriated." He paced her on the sofa and pulled a covering over her. Semiconscious, she still held on to Liam's coat.

"I'm going leave Mr. Fallows, before you feel the need to put me out again."

Charles blocked his path. "Wait, please. I'm sorry about the way I acted earlier. Thank you for seeing her safely home."

Hearing their conversation, Cassidy cringed inside. Her father sounded defeated.

"Apology accepted." Liam cleared his throat. "May I say something?"

"I guess you've earned that tonight."

Her father acceded to Liam's request. Cassidy couldn't believe it. She almost laughed. However, at the moment, nothing about her life was laughable.

"My pastor is phenomenal at family crises." He pulled his cell phone from his back pocket. "I'll call him. He can counsel you through these dark times."

An uncomfortable silence filled the room.

With one eye half opened, Cassidy saw a glassy stare on her father's face. He couldn't have hid his uncomfortable emotions even if he wanted to.

"I'm not going to talk about my personal

life with a stranger. Or have someone sit in judgment of me and my wife. We don't need a pastor for a counselor, or a counselor of any kind."

Liam threw his hands up. She imagined he must've felt one full heavy bout round with Charles Fallaws was all he could take in one day. "That's fair enough. I thought I'd offer the suggestion." He turned to leave. His hand hovered above the doorknob. "Her car is still at Bailey's. I don't know where her keys are."

"I'll take care of her car. Thank you again." He brushed the back of his hand across Cassidy's cheek. "She doesn't behave this way, just so you know. Usually, she's vibrant and alive. She's always been a sprightly little thing."

"I believe you." Liam stroked the back of his neck. "I remember her beautiful smile, and how animated she became when I gave her Karen's necklace."

Charles kneeled and laid his head on her chest. "What's happening to my little girl?" She heard him choking back emotion. "She's drowning, and I don't know how to save her."

Liam put a hand on the older man's shoulder. "Pray for her, Mr. Fallows. Through prayer, God will throw her a life jacket. That life jacket will save her through the most tumultuous waters."

Charles huffed. "Is that your answer for everything?"

Liam nodded with conviction. "Yes sir. I keep an open line to God at all times. It's worked for me." Cassidy heard his feet walking toward the door. When the alarm chirped, she knew he'd opened it. "Tonight, I'll say a little prayer for both of you." Then she heard the door close. It was second time Liam Papadakis had crossed their threshold in one day.

Cassidy wanted to scream. She wasn't asleep or comatose. Both eyes were closed, and her body refused to move. Unfortunately, her ears hadn't shut down like the rest of her body. Hearing the sadness in her father's voice took her over the edge, and deeper into the dismal abyss of depression. What was worse, she saw no way out.

CHAPTER FIVE

The next day, the sound of the doorbell sliced through Cassidy's head like a knife. Thinking was too difficult. All she wanted was peace and quiet. She'd taken some herbal sleeping pills earlier in the day. The pills were for occasional restlessness. Sometimes, painting would make her too excited to sleep. If she didn't make herself relax, she'd paint all night and day.

So far, and it was almost dinnertime, the pills hadn't worked. Despite their ineffectiveness, Cassidy lay on the sofa all day. Keeping her eyes closed, she hoped that much needed sleep would bless her with its presence.

Her father swept his feet across the hardwood floor. From the swishing sound, Cassidy could tell he was wearing his house shoes. He still wore his robe. It brushed her cheek as he walked past the sofa. The alarm chirped as he opened the front door.

"Liam." Her father sounded surprised to see him.

The sound of the man's name made her peek. The sofa was close to foyer, so she could see very well. Liam stood for a long time in front of the door. As if he was nervous, he crossed then uncrossed his arms.

"Good evening Mr. Fallows. I hope I'm not intruding." He held up Cassidy's keys. "I found these in my car this morning." Charles took the keys, without a reply. "I wanted to drop the keys off, is all. Goodbye." Liam turned to leave.

"Thank you," her father finally uttered.

Liam stopped dead in his tracks and turned to face Charles. It was if those two words her father spoke was an unspoken invitation to stay.

Her father rubbed his temples. Migraines were common with him, especially when he was stressed. Cassidy hoped he took his medicine. "I called a cab last night. Then I used her extra set to get her car home." He was being cordial. Even so, Liam was still standing on the porch.

Liam rubbed his hand down his pants as if his palms were sweaty. The bitter chill that

infiltrated through the opened door proved
that theory false. When Liam stroked his
forehead, Cassidy knew without a doubt that
he was nervous. "How is she doing today?"

Charles narrowed his eyes. "Did you
pray?"

Liam nodded.

"Well, I guess you need to pray again.
Maybe prayer is a hit or miss kinda thing. Your
plea to God didn't work." Sarcasm heavily
fused her father's voice. He opened the door
wider.

Again, she almost gave away her secret.
She wasn't asleep, yet Cassidy pretended to be
in a deep slumber.

Liam didn't wait to be invited inside.
Beneath her barely opened eyes, she saw he
brush past her father. "*I must look a mess!*" For
some reason, her appearance mattered. She
was still wearing the same clothes from the
night before, her hair disheveled.

He stepped closer to her then with a deep
breath, he leaned down. "Has she been up at
all?"

*"Where does the concern in his voice come
from?"*

Charles shook his head. "Only to go to the

restroom. She hasn't eaten at all today."

Liam kneeled closer to her to check her pupils. The putrid smell of sweat and puke undoubtedly attacked his nose. Earlier in the day, she caught a whiff of her own body. However, she refused to remedy the problem.

She heard Liam ask, "Is there a shower down here?"

With eyelids lowered, Cassidy was able to see her father's disapproval. Though she was a grown woman, evidently he still felt she was his little girl. His gesture was adoring. She almost smiled. *"Except I'm not his daughter. Not really."*

Liam sighed loudly. "I'm a cop, Mr. Fallows, not a pervert. I'm not going to undress her and give her a bath. However she does need to be cleaned up. Before I made detective, I helped street drunks all the time. A little water will get her up."

"Stop calling me drunk! I'm not drunk! I'm not even asleep!" Cassidy creased her forehead. Annoyed that Liam felt the need to fix her, and annoyed her father was entertaining him. She thought by now he would have thrown Liam out.

"Stop calling me drunk! I'm not drunk! I'm

not even asleep!" Cassidy creased her forehead. Annoyed that Liam felt the need to fix her, and annoyed her father was entertaining him. She thought by now he would have thrown Liam out.

Instead, her father scratched his head, grimaced, then acquiesced, "Her room is down the hall."

Liam picked Cassidy up and tossed her over his shoulder. "Lead the way, sir."

Immediately, her eyes shot completely opened. "Put me down!" Weakly, she swung her fists, hitting him in his back. *"Stupid pills want to start working at the wrong time!"*

Liam grabbed her around the waist and pressed her body against his. "Give me one second darling, and your wish will be my command."

"No! Put me down now!" Cassidy tried to pry his arms loose, but the more she struggled, he tightened his grip. Hearing Liam exclaim, "Wow!" Cassidy knew the moment he breached the doorway to her room.

"Just look at this room." Her room wasn't just orderly and neat. It'd taken her months to finish the Bohemian decorations. At least that was the theme she'd aimed for. Hearing how

Liam appreciated her décor quieted her. She was pleased, that he seemed pleased.

A multitude of bold colors, fabrics, and diverse patterns created a cozy environment. Eclectic art pieces, knick-knacks, ornaments and vases full of real flowers gave the room an inviting feel. Crimson velvet drapes impeded the sunlight, keeping the rays from entering. Dimly-lit Moroccan lamps hung from the ceiling. Beautiful paintings decorated every wall.

Charles entered the room and cleared his throat. "The water's ready."

"Yes sir," Liam turned toward the bathroom. "I'm coming."

Cassidy struggled again. "I'm warning you, put me down."

The shower door was already open. The water inside the shower powerfully flowed from the showerhead. Steam saturated the room. Liam didn't hesitate to put her under the stream of warm water, wetting himself in the process.

Cassidy narrowed her eyes. "How dare you!" Her voice held unmistakable anger.

He held his nose playfully, and then snickered. "Trust me, you need this."

"Get out!" She looked at both men. Her father had just let a total stranger humiliate her. "Both of you, get out!"

The men backed out of the bathroom and closed the door. Cassidy turned the water down to a slower flow, then got out of the shower to undress. Putting her ear to the door, she heard her father and Liam outside the bathroom door.

Liam's voice rang out above the running water. "This room is spectacular."

The pride in her father's voice was unmistakable. "Yeah. Everyone reacts the same way when they see her room. She decorated this space herself."

Cassidy placed her hand against the door, wishing to touch him again. Never in her life had she felt so far away from him.

"It's magical. Beautiful." Liam's voice became so low, she wondered if the words were only a private thought.

"Much like her," her father boasted.

Cassidy gasped. The love she heard in his voice was the rope she needed to climb out of the darkness. Almost, but not quite.

"Would you like to stay for dinner?" His voice grew faint and trailed off. It was obvious they were leaving her room.

"I'd love too," Liam replied, "if you don't think Cassidy will murder me."

Her father laughed. "She was pretty angry, wasn't she?"

"That's an understatement, sir."

"Sir? Military background, right?"

"Yes, Sir."

Cassidy was surprised to hear her father laugh. It wasn't his normal boisterous laugh, but it was real. When would her laughter come back? At this point, she'd even settle for a smile.

CHAPTER SIX

The next day, Cassidy sat on the sofa, wrapped in one of her mother's handmade quilts. She'd sniffed the coverlet countless times since Karen's death, trying to hold on to the woman's scent. Peony and vanilla was the only perfume she'd worn.

Cassidy heard the doorbell ring, all three times, and didn't move. Since her mother's death, she usually cried herself to sleep, thinking about her. That day she cried for different reasons. Betrayal, anger, lies. All of those negative emotions consumed her. When the doorbell rang again, she heard her father walk into the room. She didn't acknowledge his presence. Instead, she snuggled into the quilt.

Peeking from beneath the cover, she saw him inspecting her. He was probably wondering what craziness she would conjure up now.

"Did the doorbell ring?"

Rising from the sofa, Cassidy nodded. "Yes. I'll get it."

"I'll get the door sweetheart. Don't worry yourself with that."

Her eyes were probably swollen and red. Maybe her appearance scared him. She didn't turn away quick enough to hide her face. Still, she followed her father to the door.

Liam stood on the porch. He extended his hand. "Hello Mr. Fallows."

Cassidy questioned whether her father would let him in or not. She refused to eat dinner with them last night. Now she wondered what they talked about. Why was he on their front porch again? Then her father did the unbelievable. He eagerly took Liam's outstretched hand.

"After last night, please call me Charles."

"Certainly, Charles." Liam looked past Charles to Cassidy. "How are you today?"

She muttered, "There's no need for us to interact today. I've already taken a bath. Even brushed my teeth." She regretted the spiteful words as soon as she said them. Though her tone was low, she knew Liam got her message.

He recoiled. Being angry was a daily given for her now, however taking it out on other people was wrong. For that reason, she chose to isolate herself. "I'm sorry. I know you were only trying to help me."

"It's okay." Liam grinned at her. "I probably could've found a better way of getting you to take a shower. Sorry I inferred you reeked."

Cassidy knew the last remark was a joke, but she didn't have the strength to turn her frown into a smile. Instead, she looked away. There was dejection on her face, and she knew it.

For a short period of time, no one spoke.

Liam, still standing outside, heaved a loud sigh as if he was expecting something. Cassidy looked up to see that he was also fidgety. He was cracking his knuckles. She rolled her eyes and exhaled. *"Men!"*

"Dad, I think he wants to come inside."

"Of course. Where are my manners? Please forgive me. Come out of the cold." Charles stepped back from the doorway. His hospitality was a far cry from days past.

Liam wiped his boots on the porch mat before he entered. "I'm sorry to drop by like this. I've been calling both your phones all day. There was no answer. I wanted to make sure you two were okay."

Cassidy heaved a sigh. What made Liam think that less than twenty-four hours later, things would be back to normal? Things would never be normal. "What's your conclusion?"

Liam's five o'clock shadow made him even better looking. "Maybe today isn't the day, but I prayed you both find the strength to get past this."

"You prayed for us again?" Charles sounded surprised. "Why do you keep praying for us, after everything that's happened between us?"

Liam corrected Charles' statement. "I pray for you because of everything that's happened." He folded his arms. "I hope you don't mind, I spoke with my pastor about you. He believes he can help."

Charles frowned. "Thank you. We appreciate you trying to help, but we'll be fine. We don't need therapy, right Cass?" Her father didn't sound confident. He sounded scared and uncertain. Cassidy didn't respond. "Liam would you like to stay for dinner? There's more than enough."

Cassidy grimaced. Couldn't he see she was in no condition for company? She didn't want anyone, especially a stranger, to see her looking the way she did. Grieving her mother's death and lies proved too much for her to bear.

"Dad, I'm sure Liam has better things to do than hang around us," she suggested. "It's Friday. He probably has a date, or something."

Liam chuckled. "No. I'm single. I don't have a date. I'm working on it. I'd love to have dinner with you, again. Maybe tonight, Cassidy will join us."

Charles grasped Liam's shoulder firmly. "I'm not sure why our paths intersected, but I believe fate brought us together for a reason. Tonight we're getting rid of leftovers we would've had tomorrow. You're doing us a favor. We both hate leftovers."

The men chuckled and walked toward the dining room.

Cassidy didn't or couldn't move. She sighed, wondering when or if she'd ever feel whole again. Tears stung her eyes.

"Cass, honey," Charles called, "are you coming?"

Cassidy looked up. Liam and Charles stared at her. The lump in her throat impeded her speech, she swallowed hard. "Yes Dad," she whispered. "I'm coming." Her voice was so faint, she barely heard herself speak. The hoarseness in her voice and her present state must have given her away. Charles went to his daughter's side, and then held her tightly. "Give us a minute, Liam. Please make yourself at home."

"Take your time." He gave them privacy by walking into the dining room.

Taking the band from Cassidy's wrist, Charles gathered her hair, and pulled it into a ponytail. "Cass, we'll get through this somehow. I promise."

"I'm sorry Dad. How can I believe in anything or anybody? My whole life has been a complete lie. Everyone I've trusted has lied to me. Uncle Peter, Mom…" She sniffed and looked into his face. "You," she finally finished.

"You're right." Charles lifted her chin. "I owe penance for what I've done. Whatever you need to do, I'll help. I'll try to make this up to you, even if it takes the rest of my life. I can't say I'm sorry enough."

"Dad," she turned from the sincerity in his eyes. "I can't talk about this right now. We're being rude to Liam, and plus, I am hungry."

Charles' face brightened. "Fair enough."

Cassidy walked to the dining room. She heard him follow.

CHAPTER SEVEN

For the past two weeks, Liam visited the Fallows' house. Most times, Cassidy was sleeping, or staring into space. Somehow, Charles found the strength to entertain Liam. How could he possibly laugh when their life was in such disarray?

"This time she's asleep," she heard her father say.

She felt Liam sit on the sofa next to her, but she didn't stir. Why didn't he go away as he usually did?

"It's time she woke up, Charles. This madness has to end." He shook Cassidy's shoulder. "Wake up. I want to ask you something."

"Is this really necessary," she uttered, irritated that Liam disturbed her. She opened her eyes, and pulled the afghan to her chin. "Do you live here now?" As intended, her voice was combative.

Liam reached for her hand. "I know you're hurting, still you need to get off this sofa and get back to your life. Charles is willing to try therapy with my pastor. Are you also willing?"

Hearing Liam's confession, Cassidy widened her eyes. From infancy, her father had instilled a motto, what happened in their house stayed in their house. "Dad said he'd go?"

Liam kneeled on the floor before her. "Yes, he did."

Charles sat down next to Cassidy. "I asked Liam to contact his pastor on our behalf."

Cassidy winced. She couldn't believe how different her father had become since her mother died. Never had she ever seen him so docile and congenial. "You'd do that for me?"

"There's nothing I wouldn't do for you?" He kissed her cheek. "When Karen was pregnant with you, she went through months of morning sickness. She didn't care. I was overjoyed the first time we heard your fetal heartbeat. The first time you kicked inside your mother's stomach, we could hardly contain our joy. The day you were born, I sped to the hospital. Dr. Rawls didn't have to spank your bottom. As soon as you came out, you cried, taking your first breathe on your own."

"Look what my birth meant. Mom cheated."

"Your mother's sins are not your sins, Cass. After you were born, my life was never the same. No." He shook his head. "It was substantially better. Immediately, we formed an unbreakable bond. I staked my claim to you, and nothing will ever change that. For over twenty years, we've been close and inseparable. I'll do whatever it takes to fix what's broken."

Liam squeezed her hand. Cassidy was torn between the warmth of Liam's touch, and the loving words of her father. "Charles and I prayed together last night."

Cassidy frowned. She'd never seen her father prayer. Furthermore, she rarely did herself. "Dad, you prayed with Liam?"

Charles nodded. "I know we've never gone to church, except for funerals or weddings. I may not act like I believe in God, but I am a believer. You need help, Cass." He paused. "We both need help."

"I know I need help, Dad. You don't have to go with me, if you don't want to. I know you're a very private person."

Her father shook his head. "The proverbial ghost from my past came back to haunt me in the worst kind of way. The phantom skipped me and set its beady eyes upon my beloved daughter. We fight together, Cass."

Cassidy looked at Liam, and her eyes water. She couldn't find the right words to convey how amazed at him she was. "How did you get Dad to pray?"

He smiled. "I asked."

"And I was hopeless to refuse." Charles pulled a Kleenex from the box on the coffee table and gave it to her. "All I know is that this young man prays with confidence and faith. After listening to the power of his words, I wanted what he had. I'm guessing therapy would be a start. We could have prayer with his pastor. Do you want to try?"

Cassidy heaved her chest. Tears, her recently acquired trademark, rolled down her cheeks. "Yes, I want to try, Dad."

She flew into Charles' arms. That was the first time she allowed her father to embrace her. He squeezed her as if she'd never allow him that pleasure again.

After kissing her face he seemed relieved. "Oh sweetheart, that's wonderful. I really think this will help us."

"I'm so sorry, Dad. I've been so angry — blaming you for cheating and arguing with Mom. Her guilty conscience fueled her anger. How could she do this to me? To us?"

Charles hugged her even tighter. "Cass, your mom loved you. Whatever she did or didn't do, she was a wonderful mother. Hold on to that."

.

CHAPTER EIGHT

"*Why did God bring this man into our lives?*" Cassidy pondered on that question for weeks. From the moment he returned Karen's locket, she was drawn to him. He could have mailed the necklace, but he didn't. A greater power greater had commanded he return the necklace in person.

Charles was uptight with Liam in the beginning. Now they'd grown on each other. Both men shared a love of chess and played frequently.

Liam waited inside his truck for them. Cassidy hoped Pastor White could bring them closer to God. Only God could bring them out of their despair.

Charles went out of the house first. Cassidy locked the door then trailed slowly behind him. Her father seemed anxious to start their new venture. He opened the door with a hopeful expression. "Hi Liam, thanks for picking us up."

Liam flashed a brief smile. "Hello Charles. Cassidy. No need for thanks. It gives me pleasure to have you two as my guest. You're going to love my church. "

"Hi." Cassidy smiled at Liam with mock assurance. In return, Liam nodded and grinned as if to comfort her.

Charles opened the backdoor and Cassidy slid across the cool leather seats. After closing the door, Charles got into the front seat of the truck. "I have the chess board ready for a repeat of last night. That is—if you're up to a game afterwards. I've already cooked dinner, too."

"Sounds great," Liam shifted the truck into reverse, "on the other hand, I don't want to impose."

"Nonsense!" Charles chided. "Besides, last time you beat me. I should have the chance to redeem myself. I haven't had such a worthy opponent in years."

Liam laughed. "You're on. Though, don't be a sore loser. You won't win this time either. I haven't lost a chess game in years."

The thirty-minute ride gave Liam and

Charles a chance to get to know each other better. Her father did most of the talking. Every now and then, Cassidy would dab her eyes with a handkerchief. Unfortunately, Liam caught a glimpse of her in his rearview mirror. As if he wanted to comfort her, his brows were knitted. His expression was grave. *"How could he comfort me? Would I even let him?"*

There was something more about Liam. Yes, she was attracted to him physically, but... Call it his aura or his essence. Something emanated from the inside of Liam that was more appealing than his face or body.

When Liam turned into the driveway of the church, Cassidy saw an elderly man standing on the church steps. With a broad smile on his lips, his face glowed with an angelic countenance.

CHAPTER NINE

$\mathscr{F}$rom a distance, Cassidy saw the tall tower before she saw the church. The structure was imposing—a grand mixture of Gothic and classic, yet built with granite. Elaborate carvings were etched into the stone, while a steeple and spire sat atop the building. Intricate but modern designs adorned the hallowed doorway, leaving Cassidy to guess the church was erected in the nineteen hundreds. External bells chimed, announcing the time.

Liam parked the truck, then led them to the steps where Pastor White was standing. "Welcome!" he said loudly with his hands extended.

Charles offered his hand. "Thank you."

Pastor White's smile grew wider. He took Charles' hand and then, embraced him. Next, he studied Cassidy. Undoubtedly, her eyes told her story. He kissed her forehead, then hugged her. Soon, Cassidy realized his grin was infectious. To be courteous, she managed a slight grin.

"Everything will be fine," he whispered.

"Thank you for seeing us on such short notice," was all she could muster.

Pastor White greeted Liam. "Hello, Brother Papadakis."

Liam smiled and hugged the elder man. "Hello, Pastor White."

"Let's go inside." Pastor White turned and walked away, not bothering to make sure they followed.

The arched entrance opened to marbled floors. Inside, the church was large and inviting. Rows of cherry stained benches went on forever. Candles were lit. The fragrance of incense, newly cleaned instruments, and oil from the lamps mixed together. Immediately the blended scents lifted her spirit. She took a deep breath, inviting the fragrance into her body.

Detailed stained glass windows were beautiful and embellished the top of the church.

Liam grabbed Cassidy's hand. "This way."

Cassidy stopped walking and breathed in the ambience of the church once more. Pastor White and Charles waited in front of an office door. Both men looked at her, albeit differently. Charles looked worried, while Pastor White looked confident. Smiling, he took Cassidy's hand from Liam.

Pastor White placed his arm around her reassuringly. "I'll take her, Brother Papadakis. I believe the children are waiting for you in the school." He unlocked and opened his office door, then ushered Charles and Cassidy inside.

"Oh, yes. Tonight is my night to teach." Liam hesitated as if he didn't want to leave.

Pastor White went inside his office. "I'll take good care of them Brother Papadakis. I promise." He closed the door and turned to face the pair. Charles and Cassidy didn't move until the pastor pointed to two worn leather seats. "Please have a seat."

CHAPTER TEN

$\mathcal{P}$astor White's office wasn't as impressive as the sanctuary. His bookshelves were full to capacity. Books and papers were everywhere. However, the lighting was brilliant and intense. Nothing about the glow was soothing. Cassidy pondered if the wattage was purposely chosen to show everything, demons included. If so, her demons were easily discernible.

Her father twiddled his fingers and bounced his legs. Was he also uncomfortable? "How does this work?" His voice was pregnant with skepticism, and Cassidy wondered why he agreed to come.

Pastor White looked at him graciously. "First, I'd like to say a prayer, if you don't oppose."

She sat up straight. "Yes, I would like that. My friend, Jax, says prayer always helps him.

He prays all the time." Suddenly tears streaked her face. "I need help."

Pastor White sat between them and grasped Cassidy's hand. "Charles, do you want to pray with us?"

Charles hesitated. "Umm..."

She knew he was going to protest. Right then, she needed anything, including divine intervention, to help her. "Please Dad. Do it for me," Cassidy pleaded. "You said you'd meet my requirements. Daddy, I need this."

Charles reluctantly gave Pastor White his hand. He looked as if prayer would somehow chain him permanently to God. *"Even so, what's so wrong with that?"* The clergyman squeezed both their hands, and prayed fervently.

When Pastor White finished praying, he let their hands go. "Now, how can I help you?"

Charles sneered. Cassidy looked at him with irritation. He acted as if they were at a carnival sitting in front of fortuneteller. "We don't know. Aren't you supposed to ask us questions or tell us how to fix what's wrong? I thought you were the expert."

Pastor White peered over his glasses. "I can ask questions, if you'd like. However I would prefer to hear what you have in your hearts."

"I'll start," Cassidy blurted. Once she had the pastor's attention, she hesitated. *"I can do this. I have to do this."*

The minister nodded. "Go ahead, child."

She bit down on her lip, then swallowed past the imaginary lump in throat. "My entire life, my parents lied to me. I have no idea who I am."

"Cassidy!" Charles cautioned. He narrowed his eyes, and fixed his stare on her. In control at all times, he curtailed his reaction by pressing his lips into a thin line. The anguish on his face and the ire in his voice were evident. His reaction was just the spark she needed.

"What Dad? You and Mom lied to me." Cassidy hadn't seen her father's 'this is going to hurt me more than you' chastising stare since she was a teen. Back then punishment would closely ensue.

Pastor White raised his hand. "Let's go over some rules, shall we? Only one person may speak at a time. We must respect each other. No topic is off the board. And above all, no one is ever permitted to shout."

Deep burrows creased Charles' forehead.

"I'm sorry. What she said was personal and harsh."

Cassidy thought about what he'd said for a moment and she almost succumbed to his wishes. Her words may have hurt, but they were the truth. "No Dad, what you and mom did was harsh. Either we're going to do therapy the right way, or not at all. You can't control everything, Daddy."

Pastor White grabbed their hands again. "I think we need to pray, once more."

CHAPTER ELEVEN

*W*hen Cassidy and Charles walked out of the church, Charles seemed cross. However, Cassidy felt comforted. She would've been content to stay and talk with Pastor White even longer. He had held her hand and helped her break through. She hoped it was the start of overcoming her tribulations.

Pastor White kissed Cassidy's forehead. "Call me if you need to." He then shook Charles' hand. "Either of you."

* * * * *

"So Charles," Liam drove out of the parking lot. "How did therapy go?"

Charles shrugged. "I guess it was okay. Of course, I was made to be the villain. The whole session was a little too hocus-pocus for me. All he wanted to do was pray about everything."

Liam frowned. "My faith has gotten me through a lot of rough times. Prayer saved my life a time or two. I'm concerned with your choice of words, Charles. I want to be around people who share my faith, not doubters. I thought you believed in God."

Cassidy heard marked disappointment in the tone of Liam's voice.

"I do. It's just… maybe God is selective with whom he chooses to help. Look at the world. It's a mess. Why would He just decide to help me? I've never given Him anything. Why would He give to me?"

"Simply because you asked, Charles. He says, 'ask and you shall receive. Seek and you shall find. Knock and the door shall be opened.'"

"You sound just like Pastor White. Nothing is as simple as that. I don't believe we'll be going back."

Cassidy placed her hand on her father's headrest. "We're going back again, Dad." Her tone was commanding. "And again, and again." She spoke under her breath. The repeated words resounded inside the closed space of the truck.

Both men stared at her.

Liam raked his fingers through his hair. "Charles?"

Her father hesitated. "Okay. Make our next appointment."

Inwardly, Cassidy smiled. *"Cassidy one; Charles none."* She planned to help her father through the rough transitional phase, whether he wanted her to, or not.

No one said anything else on the ride home.

Cassidy walked inside the house after Charles. Before Liam could cross the threshold, she kissed his cheek. "Thank you."

Liam's body froze, and he softly gasped. His eyes looked dazed. Could her feelings for him be mutual? Pretending to tip an imaginary cowboy hat, he said, "Anytime ma'am," in a fake southern accent.

CHAPTER TWELVE

*A*lmost three weeks passed. Cassidy hadn't seen or heard from Liam, except at church. Even then, he only waved. She assumed he needed time to think. Together, they decided to give Liam some space. However, she missed him.

Tragedy had caused their paths to cross, and yet everyone needs space. Even stranger, she didn't want distance between them. She loved being around Liam.

Earlier in the day she tried calling him, but he didn't answer. When she saw his name on the caller ID, she did a happy dance. He couldn't see her, so her secret was safe.

"Hello?" she answered after one more ring. She didn't want to seem anxious.

"Hi Cassidy. I got your message. What's up?"

She beamed when she heard his voice. "Hey stranger. Dad and I were wondering if you wanted to come to dinner tonight. You've been MIA for almost three weeks. He's making lasagna. It's his specialty."

Liam paused before he answered. "Sure, give me an hour. I'll be there."

"Great. We'll see you later, right?"

When Cassidy hung up the phone she wanted to kick herself. She sounded too eager on the phone. She was getting too close to Liam, and too emotionally attached. His life was intermingled with theirs, and she didn't understand why.

CHAPTER THIRTEEN

*W*hen the doorbell rang, Cassidy rushed to the door. Looking through the peephole, she saw Liam standing on the porch. In the past, her father's disposition toward Liam had ranged anywhere between irritation to elation. Now, they both welcomed him there.

Cassidy checked her appearance in the mirror mounted near the door. Her skin glowed, and her hair was bouncy and shiny. Anxious to see Liam, she took a deep breath, then opened the door. A gray lambskin jacket, a black sweater and black slacks complimented the richness of his Greek features.

"Liam, you came." Genuine warmth filled her voice.

When Liam grinned, perfect teeth and deep dimples clouded her judgment. *"Be still my heart!"*

"I told you I was coming," he replied, taking a step forward. Secretly, Cassidy wanted to throw her arms around him, and demand that he never leave. Fear of looking like a crazed, lovesick woman, she held her arms firmly by her side. "I know. You've just been gone for so long."

Compelled by her loneness, Cassidy risked putting her arms around his neck. Immediately, Liam stiffened. Her hug must've been unexpected, on the other hand, so was his reaction. *Why is he so confused? He's probably in awe of my transformation. For once, I don't look wild. He probably feels he's looking at my doppelganger.*

"Are you okay Liam?"

"Yeah, I'm great." Liam stepped back and looked at her. "You look beautiful! I mean, really great!"

Cassidy stepped aside to let him in and flirtatiously smiled. "Beautiful is allowed." Her sudden act of boldness shocked her. It was out of her character.

Liam drew back. His eyes widened. "Then beautiful it is." He walked inside the house, then Cassidy shut the door.

Her cheeks flushed. That was the first conversation they'd had while she was rational. She couldn't mess it up. Although someone should tell that to her stomach since it was doing somersaults. Could he sense her attraction to him? Truth be known, she hoped he did.

A smug grin was plastered on his face. "I like the way our relationship has evolved."

She raised her eyebrows. "Looks like we've decided we can flirt." Cassidy was astonished by their honesty. "Come on, dinner is almost ready. Dad has been driving me crazy trying to teach me to play chess. I'm glad you're here." They started for the dining room.

Liam grunted. "Was that the only reason you invited me to dinner—so you don't have to play chess with Charles?"

Cassidy's drew in a breath and her steps faltered. She turned and gazed into his eyes. He moved closer, which in turn, made her heart sped up.

Unaware she'd held it, she expelled a breath. Was his silence a promise of things to come? Furthermore, was she reading too much into his gaze? Lord, she hoped not.

"No, Liam. I asked you to dinner because I've really missed you."

He approached her cautiously. "Cassidy, can we…"

"Hey buddy!" her father interrupted. He

had the cheesiest smile on his face. "Where've you been, man?"

The two men shook hands.

"I haven't really been anywhere." Liam's gaze strayed back to Cassidy. Her eyes never wandered from him. "Just working a case. It's been taking up a lot of my time."

"Well you're here now. That's what matters. Hope you two are hungry. I am, and I made more than enough for seconds. Let's eat." Charles appeared oblivious to their heated chemistry. He walked in the direction of the dining room. "The sooner we eat. The sooner we can play chess. This time, I'm going to win. I've come up with a few new strategies."

Liam chuckled. "Great! Can't wait." He strolled behind Charles to the dining room.

"Liam?" Cassidy gently grabbed his arm as he strode past. She heard his breath catch when he stared into her eyes. His cologne had a woody aroma. She wanted to bury her nose in his chest and inhale.

"Yes?" His voice was deep and smooth.

Cassidy swallowed and looked around the room. She focused on everything in the room, as long as they didn't linger too long on Liam. "Was there something you wanted to ask me before Dad walked in?"

Liam shook his head, and lowered his eyes. "No, it was nothing really. I just wanted you to know I'd missed you guys, too."

"That's all you wanted to say?" She let go of his arm. Her state of euphoria disappeared almost as quickly as it came.

"Yes, that was it." He walked away so quickly, that he bumped into her father.

Charles squeezed his shoulder. "Don't stay away so long, next time, buddy."

Cassidy looked away, grateful her father saved her from making a fool of herself. Now, she was frustrated. *"Did I want him to ask me out? God, please help me. Why is this so hard?"* She followed the men into the dining room, not sure where she stood with Liam.

Fortunately, her father had claimed him. He called Liam his friend.

CHAPTER FOURTEEN

*S*ix weeks of therapy and her father still hadn't fully vested himself. Pastor White cautioned that harboring regrets would eat them up inside. The man had been a Godsend, yet he still hadn't found a way to chisel the wall her father strained to uphold. Cassidy watched as he admired his well-manicured nails. He wasn't paying attention, and he rarely did.

Pastor White touched his shoulder. "Brother Fallows did you hear me?"

Charles sat up in his chair and looked at Cassidy. Racked with disapproval, she fixed a flinty stare.

"I'm sorry Pastor." He cleared his throat. "I missed your question."

Pastor White titled his head to one side. "I asked if you'd read this week's scripture? Psalms 103:2-5 says, 'Bless the Lord, O my soul, and do not forget all his benefits, who forgives all your iniquities, who heals all your diseases, who redeems your life from the Pit, who crowns you with steadfast love and mercy, who satisfies you with good as long as you live so that your youth is renewed like the eagle's.' What do those words mean to you?'"

"Honestly Pastor White, I don't know. We come here twice a week for therapy, and go to church on Sundays. Cass is progressing some, but not enough. She still has a long way to go. How long is this therapy of yours?"

The pastor stroked his chin. "As long as it takes. Charles, you can stop whenever you want."

"No!" Cassidy shouted, leaning forward. "I'm not ready to stop coming."

Pastor White patted her hand. "I meant Charles, Cassidy. You can come without him."

"Really?" Charles murmured.

Cassidy saw the flash in her father's eyes. Did her father relish never coming to therapy again? Her stomach became queasy at the thought. He was an integral part of her recovery. And though he didn't know it, she was just as important to his. "Dad, you promised me."

Pastor White raised his hand to silence her. "Charles, would you'd like to discontinue therapy?"

Not wanting to rush her father's decision, she waited anxiously.

Charles glanced at her again. She didn't blink, daring him to accept the invitation.

"No. I'm just as committed as Cassidy. I need to see where therapy leads us."

Pastor White raised both brows. "Charles, you say Cassidy has a long way to go. What about you?"

"Me?" Charles seemed astonished. "I'm great. Just peachy."

"Are you saying you no longer grieve for Karen? Or resent that she left you here to clean up her mess? And what about your best friend? Are you sure you harbor no ill feelings against him. After all, he had an affair with your wife? Are there no ill feelings against this man, even though he fathered Cassidy? All of these events make you feel 'just peachy?'"

Charles clenched his jaw and sat up in his chair. "Watch how you talk to me, Pastor White. I'm handling all of that in my own way. I always have."

Pastor White smirked.

Cassidy stood, folding her arms defiantly. "Then why are you so angry, Dad?"

He turned on Cassidy. "What do you want

to know, Cassidy? Do you want to know if I'm angry? If I hate Peter? Karen?" He stood up. "Yes, I'm angry at them. I've been angry for over twenty damn years. And yes, I hate Peter. I hate him so much, that my blood curdles every time I hear his name, or see his face." His eyes softened. "But I've never hated Karen. I loved her. I love her still."

Hearing her father's confession, Cassidy's eyes watered. "And me, Daddy? What about me?"

"You? What about you?" He lowered his brows. "Are you asking if I hate you? Cass sweetheart, please tell me you know better than to ask that question."

"I…" Cassidy started. She shrugged and tears filled her eyes.

Pastor White gave her a tissue. "Don't stop Cassidy. Tell him how you feel."

"I know you love me, Dad. I'm asking if you resent me for not being your biological daughter." Cassidy sounded apologetic, even though she'd done nothing wrong. "I'm a daily reminder of their affair. I'm a constant reminder of your hatred for Peter. What do you see when you look at me? How do you feel?" She let out a deep breath, then shamefully lowered her gaze.

Charles pulled her near. He kissed her cheek, and then brushed a stray hair from behind her ear. "I feel like God must truly love me. I must've done something right in my life, to deserve you. I also feel that if I never see you, or hold you in my arms again…" He hugged her. "My heart would shatter into pieces. I would die."

She snuggled into her father's embrace, sniffling. "Dad, you can't tell me my life doesn't bring you heartache."

"Look at me Cassidy."

She gazed into her dad's sympathetic eyes.

He brushed his thumb across her chin. Then he continued. "Karen had my heart, bur *you* are my heart. Sweetheart, I swear to you, nothing about you has ever made me feel anything other than love, pride, and gratitude. I love having you in my life. Having you for a daughter has given me joy—a joy I certainly don't deserve."

"Cassidy." Pastor White patted her empty chair. "Why did you ask your father that question?"

"I feel ashamed." Cassidy left her father's arms and then sat back down. She pulled a tissue from the box sitting on the edge of the desk.

Pastor White leaned back in his char. "Tell Charles what you mean, Cassidy."

Blotting her tears, Cassidy took a moment to speak. "Dad, when I look in the mirror, I hate what I see. I feel like a dirty little secret, or like I'm the one who doesn't deserve you."

"What? That's preposterous, Cassidy." His voice was authoritative and chastising.

"Is it Dad? For years, you've worked long hours to give me a privileged life. However, I was born and raised in a circle of lies."

Charles knelt before her. "You're wrong. You were born in a circle of love. Your birth was one of the happiest days of my life, and your mother's life as well. The lies don't matter. You were always carried in the spirit of love." He looked at Pastor White. "'And the greatest of these is love.'" I know I've read that somewhere. It's in the Bible, right?" he asked desperately.

"I Corinthians 13:13, 'And now these three remain: faith, hope and love. But the greatest of these is love.'" Pastor White indicated that Charles sit in his chair. "Come, let us pray. Our time is up. Great session this week Charles.

However, you broke a cardinal rule. You raised your voice. I'll allow that rule to be broken only once." A wide smile spread across his face.

They laughed. A warm peaceful calm flowed through Cassidy. With the mood now lifted, she felt hope. The twinkle she saw in her father's eyes told her he felt it too. The smile was still on his face.

"I won't let it happen again," he promised.

"Our ending scripture is Psalm 30:2, 'O Lord my God, I cried to you for help, and you have healed me,'" the Pastor said. "Study this scripture. We'll discuss the meaning next week." He held out his hands. Charles and Cassidy each grabbed one. "Let's pray."

Charles didn't seem to hesitate. He closed his eyes and bowed his head before Cassidy and Pastor White.

As pride rose inside her, Cassidy smiled. Finally, Pastor White was able to break through their tangled web of grief. All it took was her father's participation.

CHAPTER FIFTEEN

To say the least, the first month of therapy sessions was stressful. They told their family's dirty secrets to a complete stranger. By the third month, Pastor White had become their saving-grace. His calm demeanor reminded Cassidy of her grandmother's warm homemade apple pie, and hand-churned vanilla ice cream.

There in session, Cassidy pursed her lips. "Pastor White, how can I forgive my mother when she's not here for me to yell at?"

The gray-bearded man always sat between them, instead of behind the colossal desk. "Charles, do you feel the same way?"

Charles nodded then looked at the elder man. "We should've healed as a family years ago. Karen and I hurt each other, still what we've done to Cass is reprehensible. So yes, I wish she were here."

"Time heals all wounds. You've both come quite a long way. I'm proud of you. What else are you looking to achieve?"

"I'm looking for my happy place." Cassidy stared at the floor. "Right now, I feel so lost. Sometimes I don't know which direction is right."

Charles made a steeple with his fingertips. "Karen left me to shoulder the responsibility of a painful tragedy. My lies and infidelities didn't help either. I'm reaping what *we* sowed," he confessed. "She died, escaping the aftermath. Living with the pain is what's hard."

Cassidy held her father's hand. They were rebuilding their relationship one day at a time. "Who do you blame when the guilty party is gone?"

"God," Pastor White replied. "He is the answer for all things. Your healing is through Him. Healing wouldn't have come from Karen anyway."

"You're right." Charles lowered his voice. "Karen is gone, but we're growing in our faith, and healing."

Essentially, Cassidy believed what both men had said was true. However, it didn't negate how she'd never get to tell her mother about how she felt. Never having that possibility, she felt she'd never have complete closure. Nevertheless, her life must go on. After a few silent seconds, she took a deep breath then said, "Mom died owing me a huge debt. Weeks ago, I was angry at her. She hurt me badly. I'm not sure if I'll ever be able to forgive her. I want to. My memories of her should be filled with love, not anger."

Pastor White gave her a warm comforting smile. "But surely you have some wonderful memories of your mother? Those are the moments you need to concentrate on. Those memories define who she was."

"I have picture perfect memories of Mom brushing my hair at night. She'd also sit on the edge of my bed and tuck me in. There were lots of hugs and kisses." Emotions of love sprang inside her heart. No matter what, she knew her mother loved her.

Pastor White leaned back in his chair. "Cassidy, you'll never forget what your mother did to you, but in time you'll come to realize that only the wonderful memories count. The rest will fade into the back of your mind. You'll get there. You'll both get there."

She knew he was right. Her resentments had overshadowed loving memories of her mother. In order to fully heal, she knew she couldn't continue to allow that to happen. "I'm not where I need to be, and thankfully, I'm not where I used to be either. I can honestly say prayer changes things. Prayer is changing me." While she was talking, he gazed at the books on the shelf. They were stacked on top of each other. The pile got higher and higher each week. "What are you thinking Dad?"

He shrugged. "Honestly, the only reason I came here is because I thought I'd lose Cass. I turned to God because of a need, not a want. At first, coming here gave her such comfort. For once, she didn't cry as much. After a few weeks, she stopped wrapping herself in Karen's blanket. I came here for my daughter, and not for myself."

Pastor White drew his brows together. "And now?"

"Am I a fan of airing dirty laundry? No. But now when I go to church on Sundays, then come here for therapy twice a week, the word of God washes the dirt from my everyday life."

Cassidy flashed a grin. "I agree. The word of God cleanses me."

Pastor White appeared pleased with their answers. His proud expression pleased her. He'd waded through tough waters with them, and never complained, even when they broke the rules. And they broke those often. "Have the pupils become the teacher? You're both on the right road to healing. You're learning to forgive trespasses."

Cassidy grasped his freckled hands. When she held them, she felt comforted, even though they were dry. "What's our ending scripture for tonight?"

He removed his hands, opened his Bible, then used a book mark to pinpoint the page. "Matthew 11:28 says, 'Come to me all who are weary and burdened, and I will give you rest.'"

"Thank you Pastor." Charles placed his hand on Pastor White's shoulder. "You've given us hope. We'd never gone to church, until now."

Pastor White shook his head in disagreement. "It's not about this building, Charles. It's about what you feel inside."

"I know. Nonetheless, each time I'm here, I get a feeling of hope and love. This powerful sensation overpowers my feelings of helplessness. I also know nothing this strong could ever come from a building."

Pastor White beamed again. "I think the only thing left to say is, Amen."

In unison they replied, "Amen."

CHAPTER SIXTEEN

An hour later, they were at Liam's front door. Though they ate dinner together almost every night, it was the first time they ate at Liam's house. Snow covered the rooftop of a ranch house that sat among a few hundred scenic acres. It was nestled among a grove of aspen trees and surrounded by mountains, deer and elk roamed the land peacefully. A circular, paved driveway gave access to the property.

Over the last month, Liam and Charles constantly talked and played chess. However, Liam didn't seem to hide his interest in Cassidy. He laughed at her jokes, opened doors for her, and pulled back her chairs.

At first, Cassidy thought Liam was just being a true gentleman. On occasion, his hands lingered longer than need be. She felt the brunt of his accidental touches, while finding him quite attractive. However, his presence made her nervous.

Charles rang Liam's doorbell.

Liam opened the door, a huge grin plastered across his face. "Welcome to my humble abode." He wiped his hand on a kitchen towel. The mouthwatering aroma of food floated onto the porch.

His hair was still wet from a shower, and her heart quickened at the sight of it. His jeans hugged low, and fit him perfectly. A flannel shirt stretched across his broad chest, with the sleeves rolled up, displaying Liam's muscular arms. He was barefoot and very comfortable inside his house.

They moved into the foyer, where Liam took their coats. From there he ushered them into the living room where most of the downstairs area was easily seen. The interior was decorated with warm earthy browns, tans, and blue greens. High ceilings and an open space made the house look huge, whereas the French styled timeworn distressed tables, which were surrounded by plump ruffled sofas, still displayed a heartwarming coziness.

Charles scanned the room. He seemed impressed. "Nice home, Liam."

"Thanks. It needs a family. I'm working on

it. Please, make yourselves at home. There are hors d'oeuvres on the table, and tea or juice on the bar.

Cassidy craned her neck to take in the vaulted ceiling. "This is an awfully big house to live in. You should get a pet."

Liam winced. "I had a pet. His name was Corky." He closed his eyes briefly. "Corky was my only family."

"What do you mean?" Cassidy soften her voice. "You don't have any family."

Her father's head jerked up and quickly turned toward her. "Honey, this isn't the time, or place. We came here to enjoy Liam's company, not grill him about a painful past."

Cassidy whirled around and looked at her father. If he meant for her to change the subject, he had another thing coming. His reaction only piqued her interest even more. She persisted. "What's so painful about your past, Liam?" She sounded suspicious. "If it's too personal to share, I'll understand." Sadness came over her as she thought of a hurtful possibility. Maybe he didn't trust her. "Obviously, you've shared your life with Dad."

Immediately, Liam caught her face with

his hands. "I had this conversation a while back with Charles. It was one of the nights you didn't eat dinner with us. That's the only reason you don't know. I was orphaned at birth. I went from foster home to foster home, never staying in one place for more than a year or two. So, to answer your question, no I don't have any family."

Cassidy inhaled. There was sinking feeling in her stomach. She was relieved on one hand. Liam did trust her. However, she was conflicted on another. How could such a caring man still be alone? "Everyone has some kind of family. There's no ex-wife, or two point two kids anywhere?"

Liam chuckled. "No. I never married or settled down with anyone for long periods. Long ago, I accepted being alone. I prepared myself to accept my fate, a state of constant loneliness. You see, I thought being alone was my birthright, my curse—my personal cross to bear. Pastor White showed me I'd never been alone. God had always been with me.

Cassidy smiled. "Yes, he taught us that too."

"Knowing that I was loved by God brought me hope. The American dream of the white picket fence, and those two point five children you mentioned, began to feel within my reach. When I bought this house, I started to feel some sense of normalcy. One more step to reaching my goal. However, the house was so large, the emptiness exacerbated the truth. I was still alone. Then one day, I saw Corky in the window of the pet store." Liam grinned. "He was barking and wagging his tail at me. Corky was auditioning for a home, before I even knew I was casting a role." Liam sighed. "I loved him immediately. Finally, something loved me back. He was my dog for ten years until recently."

"Is this him?" Cassidy picked up a picture frame that encased a picture of a chocolate lab.

Liam nodded, then smiled fondly.

"Wow, ten years is a long time. He must've really been man's best friend. What happened to Corky?"

Having his lips drawn tightly, Liam looked at Cassidy's father, then he gazed at her. "Please let's sit down first. This may take a while." He sat on one of the sofas. Cassidy sat next to him and Charles sat across from them. "Well, we went camping one day. Being under the stars and fishing always relaxed Corky. He was usually so energetic and athletic. We went camping frequently so he could run around and expel some of his energy. Bad weather had been predicted. It was supposed to hit the next night, but nature has its own time. Then, the storm hit without warning."

Cassidy put the picture back down on the table in front of them. "Was he struck by lightning?"

Liam shook his head. "Racing against the wind and rain, I packed my truck. Soaked and wet, I jumped into the truck and headed home. Corky whined in the back seat. The storm made him uneasy. 'I know boy,' I told him, 'we'll be home soon. It'll be okay. Don't worry.'"

Charles picked up the picture next. "He was good looking dog. Did he jump out of the truck and somehow drown in the heavy rain when you got home? When some dogs are spooked they run."

Liam took the picture from him, and stared at it. "Not quite. It was sleeting outside the day he died. The weather made it impossible to see. We were almost home. I reached in the back to rub Corky's head. I swear I didn't blink, then out of nowhere, headlights sped straight at me.

I stepped on my brakes, to no avail. My truck, and the oncoming SUV, battled for ownership of the road. My windshield cracked, then shattered into pieces. The powerful impact threw my dog through the hole where the windshield should've been. Then, there was nothingness. Darkness took over."

Cassidy winced inwardly, and her body shook. A blush warmed her face, while a strange horror came over her. *"It can't be the same wreck!"* "How long ago did this happen?"

Liam's eyes narrowed. His body trembled. "Corky died in *our* car wreck, three months ago."

"Dear God!" Charles' placed his hand over his mouth.

Tears streamed down Cassidy's face. "Oh no, Liam. I am so sorry. Dad and I didn't know. The reports said nothing about your dog."

"No. It didn't. All anyone thought about was your mother's death."

He didn't say the words with malice, or bitterness, yet Cassidy felt as though he would've been entitled. "Mom was all over the news. That had to make your pain even greater."

Liam nodded. "It did. Every day. I must

admit. I went on an emotional rollercoaster ride when the accident first happened. There were feelings of anger, pain, loss, guilt, and lastly revenge. I felt guilty because I didn't harness Corky. That guilt was eating me alive. When I read that the wreck was caused by the weather, and the blood alcohol content of the female driver, I was livid."

Charles shook his head. The look on his face was one of shock. "The media made Karen look like the saint we all know she wasn't." Cassidy saw the pain it cause to say those words.

Liam nodded, agreeing with those horrible, but true words. "Karen was drunk. In spite of that, all the media focused on was her charity work—how she helped impoverished inner school kids—how beautiful she was as Miss Wyoming, circa 1970." He looked at Cassidy. She knew he saw what everyone saw when they looked at her. Karen. "Much like you, your mother was very beautiful. She had a glamorous face, with a smile made just for the camera. Her beauty didn't excuse her behavior, not in my eyes anyway. The media shoved the whole thing under the rug." His tone was weighted with exaggerated sarcasm.

"After all, Karen paid the ultimate price. No need to mar her good name. Three people walked away from that accident, with minor scrapes and bruises. The other casualty was a healthy ten-year-old canine. He was just a dog, so who cared? Except, I cared. I became angry and bitter."

"Liam," Charles started, then hesitated.

The men stared at each other. Cassidy saw fear in her father's eyes. *"What was he afraid of, now?"*

"Go ahead Charles, we should talk about this." Liam's gaze was fixed.

Charles flexed his fingers. For a moment he looked away, but her father had never been a coward. He looked Liam straight in the eyes. "When you returned the necklace, you had other intentions, right?"

Cassidy knew what he was afraid of. He was afraid of Liam's answer. They were friends now, even buddies. Did her father shudder to think what would've happened if the letter didn't come that day, or rather what wouldn't have happened? Liam would not be in their lives.

Liam's body stilled. His gaze was distant. They sat side by side, and she suddenly felt miles away from him. "After the car wreck, I was having nightmares. They were all too real. The recurring dreams had plagued me since the accident. Every time I saw Karen's picture, I prayed for forgiveness. Not for her, but for myself. My thoughts were vengeful. As a Christian, I knew I should pray myself past my pain, be that as it may, I couldn't. I needed to explode." He looked ashamed. "Unfortunately, you were my target, but you were out of my reach."

Charles seemed hurt. "Your anger is understandable."

Liam shook his head. "No, you don't understand. I was over the edge. I drove by your house so many times that I knew you lived six point seven miles from me, only fifteen minutes and thirty seconds away. Each time I made the impromptu drive, I looked at the odometer and clock. So many times, I wanted to knock on the door or ring the doorbell. My visit would have been considered trespassing or harassment. I needed a reason to knock on the door—a reason to get some things off my chest."

Cassidy shuddered, afraid of the far-away look in his eyes. When he squeezed her hand, she felt relieved. She knew he was venting, releasing pent up emotions. Instead of focusing on his own grief, he had chosen to help his enemy through theirs. How unselfish was that?

Charles moved to sit in the empty seat on the other side of Liam, although left some space. His reseating put Liam in the middle of them. "What happened next, son?"

"I remembered the necklace. At the hospital, a necklace belonging to one of you had inadvertently been placed among my personal belongings. Once I realized the jewelry belonged to you, the banes of my mental misery, I knew I had the golden ticket to get inside your house. The necklace was a gold heart locket. A heartfelt inscription was written to KF. It looked expensive, and I knew you'd probably want it back. Karen was in God's hands, but I felt you and Cassidy were equally to blame—you let her put the key into the ignition."

Charles searched Liam's face. Cassidy wondered what he saw there. Neither of them would've made it thus far had Liam not been there. She was also willing to bet that even with their newfound strength, neither one of them wanted him to leave.

"You were right, son," her father softly agreed. "We did let her drink and drive. I swear we didn't know she was so far gone, until it was too late. Any amount of alcohol is too much, if you plan to drive. Pastor White has taught us a lot. Go ahead and finish your story. You'll feel better."

Cassidy stiffened and hissed out a long nervous breath. Liam kissed her hand, which he was still holding. Inwardly, she simpered in disbelief. There he was again, she thought. He continued to comfort someone else although he himself was clearly in pain. She studied his face. His normally soft and relaxed facial muscles were hard and tensed. Liam apparently could tell she was apprehensive. He grinned at her like there was nothing to worry about before continuing.

"Well. I scooped the rental car keys off my dresser and rushed into the kitchen. My cell phone was on the table, and my Bible was there too. I wondered if God was beckoning me. I was ashamed of my thoughts. I picked up the Bible, and suddenly my chest felt so heavy. I wasn't a vengeful man, nor did I want to become one. Then, I realized I wasn't at war with either of you. I was at war with myself.

Seemed as if a little imp sat on my shoulders; coaxing me to act foolish. Pastor White sat on the other shoulder commanding me to do the right thing. The strength of Pastor White's prayers won. I threw the keys back on the table, and called him. After three weeks of prayer my soul finally settled. That's how I know prayer changes things. I'm a living testimony."

Cassidy smiled widely at him. When she looked directly into his intense eyes, she felt as if she could fall into them. God help her she wanted to. As inappropriate as her thoughts were at the moment, she couldn't help but find the thought tempting. Instead, she swallowed hard and gave him another smile. This one much was smaller. "I'm glad God gave you the courage you needed. We would still be lost had you not."

Liam smiled back at her, then to her father. "Thank you both for listening to me."

With a guilt-ridden face, she caressed his arm. "That's the least we could do for you. You lost your family that night, too."

Charles gripped Liam's other arm. "We didn't know, son. I'm sorry for your loss."

"Thank you. I miss Corky. He was my only

family. I never felt alone when he was with me. I'm relieved he died instantly in the wreck. I was assured he felt nothing. Thank God."

Liam relaxed his wide shoulders and let out a sigh. He looked relieved. Cassidy had an epiphany. This was the first time she'd seen his shoulders rounded. They were normally always squared. She previously thought it was because of his military background. Now, she believed the wreck, Corky's death, her mother, her father and herself were the causes of the tenseness in his body.

"You're not alone anymore," Charles said soothingly. "You have us. We are your family now, and *you* are ours."

Cassidy felt they should do more, a memorial of sorts. "Did you bury him in the pet cemetery?"

He nodded. "He's in the pet section of the same cemetery where you buried your mother."

"We should go visit him, if you're okay with that. Let's put flowers on his grave and say a prayer."

Liam beamed. "Of course, we're family."

"Yes we are, son." Charles' stomach growled, and they laughed. "Guess I can't hide that I'm hungry. Dinner smells wonderful."

Liam smiled. "You smell my specialty—sausage and pepper baked ziti."

Cassidy noticed the deliberate shift in conversation. Her father tried to bring light back into the room. They survived the wreckage. It was time they changed directions. She stood and wandered about the room, then nudged her father and pointed to some paintings on the wall. Those were her paintings. She'd know her work anywhere.

Charles snickered. "Are you an art enthusiast, Liam?"

"Not really. I love paintings, but I wouldn't know a Monet, from a Rembrandt. Are you referring to the paintings on the walls?"

"Yes." Charles nodded. "They're very nice."

Cassidy secretly slapped his arm.

"I bought them from the Panache Art Gallery downtown. One of the artists supposedly lives here."

"He really doesn't know these paintings are mine!" Cassidy cleared her throat to keep from laughing. "Dad and I are going to an art exhibit at Panache this weekend. Would you like to join us?"

Liam poured a glass of tea and gave the

glass to her. "I'd love to go."

Charles poured himself a glass of tea. He'd stopped drinking as much alcohol since the wreck. "I'm glad you can go Liam, because I can't. I have a business proposal due on Monday, and I'm not nearly finished."

Liam gave her a cocky smile. "Well Cass, I guess it's a date then."

She took a long gulp of the iced tea. "It won't be considered a date."

After squeezing a lemon slice into his tea, Liam took a sip to hide his grin. "Sorry, I'll rephrase that. I would love to go on this non-date with you Cassidy. What time should I pick you up?"

"Actually, I'll pick you up."

He blinked at her as if surprised. "You're picking me up?"

She nodded.

"Why? You're not into men being chivalrous. Or are you still proving we won't actually be on a date?"

"I'd love to go on a date with a chivalrous man," she replied. "However, you and I aren't going on a date."

Her father laughed loudly. It was his normal, eyes crinkling, mouth so wide the corners almost reached his eyes, kind of laugh. Cassidy was relieved to hear it again.

Liam furrowed his brows. "So I've heard." A timer went off in the kitchen. "I believe our dinner's ready."

CHAPTER SEVENTEEN

*J*ax, the owner of the art gallery, sent a limousine to pick Cassidy up. She stood outside Liam's front door, nervously ringing the doorbell. It had been a months since she been in a relationship. Usually she didn't miss the company, though something about Liam made her hopeful in the future.

He stepped out of the house wearing a black tux, tie, vest, white shirt and black shoes. He also wore a long black overcoat over his suit. On Liam the suit was anything but typical. While they walked toward the limousine, a cool breeze blew his expensive cologne past her nose. "Wow," Liam marveled, "this is more than I expected."

"Is the limo too much?"

Liam stared at her. "Actually, I'm talking about you. You're beautiful tonight."

Her cheeks felt warm. "Thank you." She looked at him, and he stared back at her through his impossibly long eyelashes.

Sometimes, the chemistry between them was electrifying. Right then was one of those times. She bit her lips nervously. "I must admit. You took me by surprise."

"Am I allowed to comment on your beauty?" His voice was neutral. "I wasn't sure, since this isn't an actual date."

"Yes," she replied hoarsely. "I just said you looked nice."

"Thank you." He straightened his suit comically. "I heard I clean up pretty good." He melted her heart with a smile. "However you, Cassidy Fallows, are simply breathtaking."

She refused to meet Liam's eyes again and pulled at the hem of her dress. Though she was flattered, she was uncomfortable with the way he looked at her. Her strapless taffeta black sheath was tastefully form-fitting, yet revealed her long legs and sculpted arms. Her white, knee-length wool coat didn't hide much else, which was her intention until then. In that moment, being under his scrutiny, she wasn't feeling so brave.

"We should get going. I don't want to be late." Cassidy slid nimbly into the limo, giving Liam an unrestricted view of her legs.

She wondered what he'd think when he

saw her with the coat off. The back of her dress was cut low. Years of exercise had made her back one of her most striking features. Liam was no different than any other man. She saw the way he appraised her legs.

"Wow!" He slid into the limousine after her. "I don't think I've ever had a date so gorgeous and graceful."

She turned from his view. A bittersweet thrill coursed through her body. "Liam this isn't a date, remember?" Cautiously, she turned to face him. "You need to accept this for what it is. Don't read anything extra into it."

He pressed his lips together. They were crimson and full. Cassidy turned away again. Liam was very easy on the eyes, and she was only human.

"Okay." Liam was quiet for a while, as if deciding his next move. "If I ask you to breakfast tomorrow morning, and you agree to go with me, will that be considered a date?"

"No, it'll be considered breakfast." His question startled her. Why was he pushing this? Pursuing her? Unable to look at him any longer, she gazed out the window. As the limo made its way to the affair, Cassidy toyed with an imaginary spot on her dress.

Liam placed his hand on top of hers. "And if I'm willing to take things as slowly as you want?"

Her heart beat wildly inside her chest, she felt open and on display. Cassidy removed his hand and stared past presence. "You'd probably become an old man waiting for me."

His humor vanished. His gaze became intense. "Cassidy, are you attracted to me at all?"

With a deep sigh, Cassidy reinforced her resolve, though still not directly looking at him. Her answer would either give him false hope, or hurt his feelings. Liam was good to her. She didn't want to do either. However, she owed him honesty.

"Yes, I'm attracted to you. I'm also attracted to bees stealing nectar from a flower. Pollination always fascinated me, still I know not to engage the bee lest the bee stings me."

His jaws tightened. "I'm guessing you've been stung before?"

"Repeatedly," she replied. "Not to mention, I have trust issues. My whole life has been a lie. I need to believe in the sanctity of love and marriage. I thought my parents were in love. They lived a lie. What I thought was love, wasn't."

"I'm going to give you time Cassidy, but I'm not giving up. It's time you took the stingers out, and allow your wounds to heal. Love is different for everyone. What your parents accepted as love may have been enough for them. You have to find what will make you happy. I believe I can give you what you seek."

"Maybe you can." She cast her eyes downward. "I'm not sure I'm ready to try just yet."

"Then I'll wait."

Fear coiled inside her. Her breath hitched. "Why would you do that?"

He shrugged. "I'll wait for you because I want to be with you. I think you're ready for a relationship. What if we're made for each other? You're just scared. I won't hurt you, Cassidy."

Exasperated that he wouldn't accept their fate, she shook her head. "Liam. Can we please talk about something else? Anything else will do."

The limo stopped in front of the art gallery. In front of the door an easel with a large picture of Cassidy herald her arrival. Surprise and disbelief spread across Liam's face.

He half-grinned, then it turned into a dazzling smile. "You didn't tell me this was *your* exhibit." He looked at the easel again, then the media clamoring by the limo. "Why didn't you tell me you were an artist?"

Despite their previous conversation, Cassidy laughed. "You don't frequent the art world, do you? I'm somewhat of a celebrity in this world. Don't you remember when we first met? I had paint on my face. Anyway, what did you think I did for a living?"

A blush swept across Liam's cheeks. "In this economy, I assumed you were just unemployed. There's no excuse. I should've asked."

Cassidy looked up, finally able to safely gaze at him. "No. I should've opened up to you more — at least about my occupation. You own four of my paintings."

He snorted, and his cheeks colored. "You and Charles must've had a good laugh."

"No, Liam. I was truly flattered. Dad and I both respect and appreciate you. We'd only laugh with you, never at you." She touched his cheek. "Do you want to leave?"

Liam glanced out the window. He laced

his hands together and placed them on his lap. Their limo driver stood by the door and waited. Photographers and the media circus clamored to swarm over Cassidy. He leaned forward and straightened his tie.

"Absolutely not! I'm going to be the envy of every man in this town." He offered her his hand. She paused, then took his hand. Liam knocked on the window to signal the driver they were ready to exit the vehicle.

"Tomorrow the media will have you as either my new beau, or boy toy," she warned.

"I'd prefer being perceived as your beau. At this point, I'll take either one. If I'm lucky, some might even believe what they read."

Cassidy laughed again. It felt good to feel some sense of happiness, even if the cheer was sporadic. "Let's get out Casanova, before you make me late for my own exhibit."

CHAPTER EIGHTEEN

*H*ours after they arrived at the gallery, Cassidy marveled at how perfectly Liam fit into her world. He was charismatic and cordial. Her friends, especially Jax Beauregard, the metrosexual owner of gallery, crowded around him. Champagne flutes were kept full, and her paintings kept selling.

Benefactors and potential buyers flocked to her because she was the exhibiting artist. Smiling and shaking hands came with the territory, a task Cassidy had generously accepted. However, that time, everyone wanted to dolefully hug her and give her condolences. All night long people unwittingly reminded her of the weighty endowment of pain she inherited from Karen. Just when she thought her night couldn't get any worse, Peter Hass walked into the gallery.

Why did his being there surprise her? He'd always come to her art exhibits. Had his visits only been an excuse to see Karen?

Notwithstanding, Peter was also always very punctual and the doors opened hours earlier. Cassidy felt she'd dodged a bullet.

But there he was, as always, walking around and proudly commenting on her paintings. The bullet felt lodged in her heart. Now, his brazen attitude angered her. Even more, his presumptuous parental actions made her sick to her stomach.

After admiring a painting, Peter looked up. For a split second, their eyes met. Cassidy wanted to run, but the insensible stilettos on her feet made her withdraw that decision. She had avoided his phone calls and when he rang the doorbell, neither she nor Charles bothered to answer the door.

Peter started in her direction once again and Cassidy flinched. She wasn't ready to confront him. Not without Charles, her knight in shining armor. A woman she didn't recognize stopped him to talk. Cassidy closed her eyes, grateful to God for the reprieve.

"Thank you Lord," she whispered.

Jax witnessed the exchange. He grabbed her hand and pulled her into a corner.

"Spill," he demanded. "What's going on between you and that repulsive Peter Hass?"

White Tulips

The dress attire was black and white formal. Jax wore an expensive red tux. He stood out from everyone else. He always did. More like Ascot Ball versus the prom, except no man or woman in the room looked better than him. His silk tailor-made designer suit wouldn't fit anyone's frame but his.

Jax was average height and thin. He had muscles, however unless he was in casual clothing, which wasn't often, his muscles were hidden. He was a very handsome man with electric blue eyes. Bronze highlights, adorned his long, wavy, perfectly coifed hair.

Cassidy often joked with him how he'd never get married because he looked better than any woman. Who could compete with that? What woman would want to?

"I can't see him right now Jax," she finally said. "Mom is gone and…" Her voice trailed off.

He put his finger against her lips. "Honey, tell me later. Do you need me to run interference for you?"

"Yes." Cassidy's voice was broken.

"Cass, you don't have to stay here all night, honey. I can make excuses for you."

Cassidy kissed his fragrant cheek. "Thanks

Jax."

He pointed to his other cheek. "One more?"

Cassidy smiled and kissed his other cheek. "Anytime."

He cracked his knuckles. "Showtime!" he said, with a sneaky grin. "Keeping Peter Haas away from the beautiful Cassidy Fallows, coming up." Jax fixed his suit coat and strode over to Peter. After grabbing his arm, they walked in the other direction.

Cassidy was touched. Having Jax as her manager had been the best career decision she'd ever made. Having him as her best friend was one the greatest blessings God had ever bestowed upon her.

*****

Cassidy crept inside an empty office. She took off her shoes to rub her feet. When Liam opened the door, she jumped with surprise.

He kneeled before her and took up the task of being her masseuse. "Are you trying to sneak away from your own exhibit?"

"It's only nine o'clock," she complained. "I have an hour left to smile and mingle. I don't think I can stay another thirty seconds. Peter keeps trying to talk to me."

Liam stopped massaging her foot. "He's

here?"

Cassidy nodded. "Jax is doing a great job of keeping him away from me, but it's just a matter of time. I'm only prolonging the inevitable."

"What do you want to do?"

"I don't know, Liam. This isn't just about Peter. If one more person offers me condolences, or asks me how I'm holding up, I'll start screaming."

"Let's just leave. Jax told me to take you home." He picked up her shoes. "The limousine is waiting for us."

Cassidy stood up, lost her balance and tumbled into Liam's chest. Her body heated instantly by the unexpected contact. "Oh, I'm sorry." Their impassioned chemistry soared, leaving her breathless.

Liam leaned in and gently kissed her lips. "I'm not. It's the only way I've been able to have you in my arms." He tightened his embrace.

She placed her hands on his chest, trying to put distance between them. Liam loosened his grip.

"Liam," she said, apologetically. "I'm not sorry you kissed me, and I'm not saying I wouldn't love for you to kiss me again—someday. Right now, I need time."

"Fair enough. I'm not going anywhere though." He wrapped her in his arms.

"I'm slowly realizing that I don't want you to go anywhere." Cassidy looked up at him. "But I do want to get out of here," she said with a smile.

Liam grabbed her hand, and then led her out of the office. Covertly, he looked around the gallery. "Come on."

They dashed toward the exit.

CHAPTER NINETEEN

*A*t home, Cassidy soaked in a hot bath to put her in a better mood. The water soothed her tense muscles. An oversized t-shirt and lounging pajamas hung on the back of the bathroom door. "Wear me," they seemed to say. She listened, adding warm fuzzy socks to the comfortable ensemble.

The bath relaxed her nerves but, as the clock struck closer to ten thirty, her mood started to sour. After her exhibits, Peter usually came by their house to give her congratulatory white tulips, Karen's favorite flowers. Cassidy hoped and prayed that night, he'd skip the tradition.

Cassidy smiled as she walked into the living room where Liam and her father played chess. The picture perfect moment of their interaction warmed her heart. Charles lent Liam a button down shirt and a pair of jeans. She sighed. Whatever the man wore always looked great on him.

When she looked at her father, she frowned. Beads of sweat were on his forehead. The heat was off and only the fireplace was lit. Why was he sweating? She sat on the side of his chair and pressed her hand against his forehead.

"Dad, are you okay? I hope you aren't catching a cold."

He yawned. "I think I'm just tired. I'm going to turn in after this game. Liam, you're welcome to stay in one of the guest rooms. Cass or I can take you home in the morning."

"That sounds great." Liam stretched his arms over his head. "I'm a little tired myself. I could use some sleep." He widened his eyes. "If Cassidy wants to make us a cup of hot chocolate we could talk for a while. I would forego days of sleep for cocoa, and Cassidy." He sounded hopeful.

She laughed, rose and went to the refrigerator behind the bar. Then she grabbed a cold bottle of water and gave it to her father. After leaning toward Liam's ear, she whispered, "Cassidy just might." He seemed to bring out the fiery bold side of her.

Liam flinched and ran his fingers threw his hair. She must've surprised him with her forwardness. Cassidy smiled. She liked knowing she could make him squirm a little. It made her feel in control again, almost like her former confident self.

"Okay you two," her father said, chuckling. "I can take a hint. Three is a crowd." He downed the bottle of water. "Let me win this game Cass, and he's all yours."

Liam laughed. "Check," he said, enthusiastically.

Charles grinned. "I can't ever beat you." The doorbell rang. He looked at Cassidy with a scowl on his face. "He's quite predictable. Isn't he?"

"I'll get the door," she said, exhaling. "Finish your game."

Liam moved his rook. "We're already finished. Checkmate." He looked at Charles. "Who's predictable?"

Cassidy looked into the peephole. "Ugh!"

Peter was on the porch.

"Is it him?" Charles' voice was thick with irritation.

She nodded.

"You don't have to open the door, sweetheart."

Liam looked confused. "Who's at the

door?"

"He knows we're here. You know how he is. He won't leave. Let's just see what he wants," she said, before she opened the door.

Not waiting to be invited, Peter walked inside. His personality had always been domineering. Right then he rubbed her the wrong way. "Sure, just come right in."

He kissed her cheek before giving her a bouquet of white tulips. Cassidy wiped away the kiss, feeling as if she needed another bath. Nausea gripped her stomach. The throbbing pain at her temples told her the onset of a migraine was surfacing. Peter's presence threatened to send her blood pressure through the roof. She put the box of flowers on the sofa, making a mental note to put them in the trash.

"Cassidy, I'm sorry I was late for the exhibit. I kept trying to talk with you, but Jax was very talkative tonight. Funny. Before tonight, I never really thought he liked me that much."

She rolled her eyes. "Yeah, that is funny. Who in the world could possibly have a distaste of you?" The remark went right over Peter's head. He looked delighted as if she'd given him a complement.

"Honey, Jax said you left early. Why would you leave your own exhibit? It's rude."

She folded her arms. "I'm not a child anymore. I come and go as I please."

"I know you're not a child anymore," Peter said proudly. "I was there when you were born." Charles pushed his chair back and stood. The noise drew Peter's attention. "Hello Charles. I don't believe I saw you at our girl's exhibit tonight."

Charles snorted. Another scowl adorned his face. "No Pete, I wasn't able to attend *my* daughter's exhibit tonight."

The tiny muscles around Charles' temples pulsed. His lips curled with contempt. Peter unnerved him, and without trying. Cassidy searched Liam's face. Did he also see the hostility on her father's face? He was about to erupt. The situation needed to be diffused.

Liam extended his hand to Peter. "I took his place tonight," he said. "I'm Liam Papadakis."

Peter barely shook Liam's hand. "Peter Hass." He looked from Cassidy to Charles. "What's going on with you two? I haven't seen or heard from either of you in months. Neither of you have returned any of my phone calls."

Cassidy took Peter's hand and led him to the door, cringing with every step. She was disgusted just by touching him, but she did it for Charles. "We were just about to turn in. One of us will call you tomorrow."

Peter jerked his arm away. "No, something is going on. I'm not leaving here until one of you tells me what it is."

Charles towered over Peter, who was five eleven at most. "Now isn't the time, Peter."

"It's okay, Dad." Cassidy gently touched her father's arm. "Now is just as good a time as any, but tonight you don't feel well. Let me do the honors."

Liam looked at her with pleading eyes, although it was too late. Peter's refusal to leave fueled the tiny spark inside her which teetered on becoming a raging fire.

Peter went to the bar and poured himself a glass of vodka. "What are you two talking about?"

Cassidy put her hands on her hips as she mentally prepared herself. The confrontation was a belated necessity. "We're talking about the affair you and Mom had. Of which, I'm the result."

Peter spewed his drink, and it drizzled

onto his clothes. He was dressed impeccably, as always, and in an expensive tuxedo. He picked up a napkin and tried frantically to clean his suit before addressing her accusation; then he took a long sip from his glass. "Who told you?"

Cassidy sneered. He didn't even have the decency to deny the accusation. "You did, just now."

Peter leaned against the bar, emotionless, pouring himself another drink. "I loved Karen. I wanted us to become a family. I asked countless times for her to divorce Charles and marry me. She wouldn't."

Her father clenched his jaws. "You stupid son of a…"

Cassidy grabbed his hand, controlling his anger for the moment. If she didn't get Peter out of their house soon, she wouldn't be responsible for her father's actions. "Peter, Mom never divorced Dad because she loved him. So you never married nor had children, waiting for her."

Peter's eyes never wavered. "I did have a child Cassidy—you. I was there at your birth, maybe not in the delivery room, but I was at the hospital. From that day on, I've never left your side. Now either you continue to call me Uncle Peter, or I'd prefer Dad, but don't ever address me as just Peter again."

Cassidy glared at him. "Then I won't address you at all, because you aren't my uncle or my father. You've had borrowed glimpses into my life. No man, other than my father, has ever been there for me." She looked longingly at Liam. *Except for you, Liam.* Cassidy hoped her eyes conveyed what she couldn't say. She hugged her father's waist. "This is my father. God joined us together, not DNA."

Peter put his drink on the bar. "No matter how much you want him to be your father, he's not nor will he ever be."

Charles stood directly in front of Peter.

"Dad," Cassidy said, touching his arm again. This time he shrugged. The reprieve was over. He was in full breach.

"Your DNA doesn't make you her father, Pete." His voice was steely. "You were just my sperm donor. You walked in and out of her life at will. Karen and I made decisions for Cassidy, not you. Karen didn't want you to be her father. That's why she stayed with me. My daughter has never been anything to you except something of a trophy, just like Karen was. Your hobby was collecting what was mine."

"You're not her father!" Peter pressed his lips together. "I am."

"And what, Karen wasn't my wife either? You fool! You've coveted everything that was mine. All I ever had to do was love them both, which I did wholeheartedly. I made mistakes with Karen. I can't ever correct that. At any rate, I'll spend the rest of my life making them up to Cass, my daughter!"

Liam stood between the two men. He towered over Peter too, but he only had a few inches over Charles. They were almost neck and neck. "Fatherhood is being responsible for another. A father is a man who exercises paternal care over another," he said. "DNA doesn't have to match."

Peter poignantly frowned at Liam. "Who are you again?"

"That's irrelevant," Liam replied.

Cassidy saw a menacing smile spread across Liam's face. His unblinking stare seemed to dare the smaller man to become confrontational. *"Not helping Liam!"* She gave him a quick angry look. How can he keep Charles calm if he became riled? *"Dear Lord, I could use a little help here please!*

Peter squirmed uncomfortably, then stepped back. He seemed unsure of whether he wanted to tangle with such a giant of a man. Her father open and closed his fists.

"After fifty years of friendship, this is what we're reduced to, Charles?" His voice was low. "Fighting won't change what happened. Karen would still be the love of my life and Cassidy will still be *my* daughter."

Veins popped out in the sides of Charles' neck. "I'm warning you. Shut up Pete."

"Or, what Charlie?"

"Oh no!" Cassidy yelled in her mind. She knew her father wouldn't be able to stop himself. Not with Peter's antagonisms. Cassidy flinched, knowing the exact moment he decided to attack Peter.

A scream tore from her lips. "Dad, no!" She was a little too late.

Her father flew into Peter at full speed, slamming into his body. He struck Peter's face over and over again until his face was bloody. She looked desperately at Liam. Why was he allowing that to happen? "Stop this!"

"Cassidy, trust me when I say that your father needs to do this. I'm an officer of the law and a man of God, so yes I should stop this. But I am also a man, and Charles' friend. This rage inside him, inside them both, needs to be appeased somehow. Otherwise, it'll destroy them and make them remain bitter inside. I won't let it get out of hand."

"It already is out of hand," she yelled, sprinting over to the fighting men. "Dad, please stop this!"

After just a few seconds, he was out of breath which worried her. Her father was in peak condition and ran five miles most days. Why was he panting so hard?

Blood spewed from Peter's mouth and nose. "Is that all you got, Charlie?"

"I think that's enough!" Liam grabbed Peter's arm, trying to get him away from Charles. "Both of you have gotten things off your chest. It's time to let bygones, be bygones.

Cassidy narrowed her eyes. "You should leave, Peter. Don't dangle raw meat in front of a hungry lion."

"Oh, who's afraid of the big bad Charles?" He jerked his arm from Liam. "Going barbaric is beneath me. I thought it was beneath you too, Charlie," Peter yelled. "What, with your refined upbringing and all. Mrs. Mary would be so proud!" Peter spat on the floor. His spittle was mixed with blood. "You're nothing more than a common thug!"

The mention of Cassidy's grandmother made her gasp. The saintly woman who was now long deceased, had doted on her as well as Charles.

Peter collapsed to the floor and Charles followed him. He closed his hands tightly around the smaller man's neck, hesitating for only a moment, then he squeezed.

"Charles no! Let him go." Liam tried to pry Charles' fingers from around Peter's neck. The more he tried, it seemed the harder Charles squeezed.

"Don't tempt me, Pete. You're not fit to hiccup my mother's name, let alone say it with such a straight face. At this moment, I'm holding on by a very thin thread. You don't know what I'm capable of doing."

Her father behaved like a crazed man. Cassidy had never seen him so angry, and so out of control. "Stop, Dad! Let him go."

Liam had gotten one of Charles' hands from around Peter's neck. Yet he still struggled with the other. "Charles, you know I can't let you do this." He glared down at Peter. "Even though Peter deserves this and more," he added. "'Vengeance is mine', said the Lord. This battle is not yours, man. This battle belongs to God."

Charles didn't let go. "I'm not there with you, Liam. God has a lot of work to do."

Liam panted, and sweated as if he'd just run a marathon. He should've been a hostage negotiator. His demeanor was calm as he tried to talk his chess partner down. "You've committed your life to God. That's not a promise you want to easily break. Exodus 20:13, The Sixth Commandment states, 'Thou shall not kill.'"

Cassidy sobbed. "Dad, please let him go."

Charles took a deep breath, and then slowly released Peter. "You're right. I am a child of God." He and Liam both fell to the floor, exhausted.

"Man, are you crazy?" Peter shouted, between bouts of coughing. He grabbed his throat. "Why are you just now saying something? It's been more than twenty years. Why did you wait until Karen died? We knew you knew, Charlie. Why didn't you say anything? Were you afraid she'd leave you?"

Charles froze.

The dark fierce stare on his face frightened Cassidy. She wondered if the revelation stung him. He sunk, as if the fight in him left. She knew at that moment, Pastor's White's symbolic Berlin wall must have finally come crashing down. All that remained was the look of pain on his face.

"I loved her, Pete. There's no other reason. I loved her and my daughter so much, that I sacrificed a piece of my sanity to keep them."

Peter's hands trembled. "You mean my daughter. I sacrificed too. Karen held both decks of cards, yours and mine."

Tears ran down Charles' face. She watched her father unravel more and more with each passing second. "How long did the affair go on?"

Cassidy looked at Peter. She wanted to know the answer, too. He diverted his eyes. Did he feel remorse?

"Until Cassidy was about eight." Peter's voice was almost an inaudible whisper. "Karen grew afraid when she became aware you knew about us. She thought you'd leave her. Imagine my devastation, when she broke off our affair to save her marriage. She didn't even care that you cheated, thinking she deserved all of your infidelities." He huffed with repulsion. "Karen didn't want you to leave her. But I never stopped hoping she'd remember how much I loved her. From our love, Cassidy was created. I wanted her to leave you and be with me!"

Charles wiped his eyes. "Well don't mince your words, Pete. Tell me how you really feel." He tried to flex his hand, and flinched.

Cassidy ran behind the bar to get a bag of ice. Ice would help some. By morning though, his hand would still be swollen. She came from behind the bar. Seeing Charles crying, she stopped midstride. He sobbed uncontrollably. He was such a strong man. Right then he seemed defenseless. It was a side of him she never knew.

"When we were kids, I shared everything with you Pete. As men, though unwittingly, I even shared my wife." His voice faltered. "I won't share Cassidy. She's mine," he said as a finale.

A tear fell from Peter's eyes. "She's never been yours, Charlie. Cassidy is a Hass, not a Fallow."

Cassidy ran to her father's defense. Liam stopped her. He whispered in her ear. "He needs to let these demons out."

Charles got off the floor. "Our dark time together was seasonal, Pete. Light is shining upon me now. Unless you find God and ask for his forgiveness, I'm quite sure darkness will forever surround you."

"Don't talk to me about God, Charlie," Peter yelled, sounding disgusted. "I haven't been a fan of His since my father lost his job. When I was a child, we had to eat from your family's table. Then, when I was thirteen, He took my mother away."

"That's blasphemous, Pete. At least you didn't go hungry, and He replaced your mother with mine. My mother loved you as if you were hers. I've had all that I'm prepared to take from you ever again. It's time for you to leave."

Peter turned on the faucet behind the bar, soaking a napkin to clean his bloody face. "Understand Charlie, our time was up many, many years ago. You held on to us, not me. And you can't speak for Cassidy."

"Get out of my house, Pete." Charles was calm. He wasn't crying anymore. The tracks of salty tears had stained his face. "Next time, only God himself will be able to pull me off you."

"Leave him alone, Peter," Cassidy said. "Haven't you and Mom done enough?"

Peter grabbed her hand. "Please talk to me. We need to talk about this. I'm ecstatic, you know. Do you know how long I've wanted to shout to the world that you were mine, and not his?"

She jerked her hand from his grasp. "You'll never be my father! I already have a father, the very best father."

Her father put his arm around her.

"Charlie, you can't just shut me out of her life."

Cassidy raised her chin defiantly. "No, but I can shut you out of my life."

Her father opened the front door. "And I can shut you out of my house." His breathing was erratic as he grabbed Peter's arm. "Get out Pet…" He stopped shouting, clutched his chest and fell to the floor.

Cassidy dropped the bag of ice. "Daddy!"

Liam picked up the phone, and dialed 911.

"Daddy," she called frantically, "what's wrong?"

Liam kneeled next to them, his family. "Charles, the ambulance is on its way. Stay with us, buddy."

"Oh, please Charles," Peter said with an exasperated sigh. "Is this the best you can do?"

Cassidy glared at him. "I don't know what Mom could have possibly seen in you. You have nothing I want, or need. Just leave us alone. Dad and I are the victims here. You and Mom don't get to hurt us ever again." She wiped her face with the back of her hand. "Those were the last tears I'll ever shed because of you. Get the hell out!" she screamed between clenched teeth. "Make no mistake Peter. Neither of us wants you in our lives anymore."

Cassidy saw Liam flinch. The cold loathing tone of her voice must've have chilled his bones.

As if her words wounded him worse than Charles' fists, Peter stiffened. Tears fell from his eyes, and blood still ran from his nose. "Cassidy, you can't mean that."

Kneeling on the floor, she stroked Charles' hair. "Liam, Peter has been asked to leave these premises repeatedly. Make him go away, please." Her voice was harsh and cold. The cruelty to her tone surprised even her.

Liam addressed Peter. "Earlier, you asked me who I was." He pulled a police shield from his pocket. "My name is Detective Liam Papadakis. If you linger a second longer, I'll have you arrested for trespassing."

Peter walked to the door, then turned. He looked at Charles. "I'm sorry, Charlie. I know I haven't been a very good friend to you." He then looked at Cassidy. "She needs you. Stay here for her." Peter opened the door. "I'll call the hospital to check on you."

"Please!" Cassidy scoffed. "If you'd had your way, he'd be six feet under already. Get out!"

"Sweetheart," Charles said, weakly reaching for her hand.

She squeezed his hand. "Daddy, I'm here."

He gave her a weak smile. "I love you, Cass."

"Daddy, please don't leave me."

Sirens wailed as the ambulance pulled into their driveway. Peter left the front door open, giving the paramedics access.

CHAPTER TWENTY

Sitting in a hospital room conjured up memories for Cassidy. She held Charles' hand firmly. He'd done the same for her whenever she was sick.

Liam walked into the room. "How's he doing?"

"How'd you get into ICU?"

He shrugged. "I told them he was my father-in-law." She shook her head, flabbergasted.

"What? It could happen," he said. "Anyway, I'm working on it."

"Good," Charles said hoarsely, "because I long to walk my beautiful daughter down the aisle."

"Hi Daddy." Cassidy kissed his cheek. "How do you feel?"

"I feel like I had a heart attack."

"Well you didn't. You had atrial fibrillation, not a heart attack. What could possibly have you so stressed?"

Charles held her hand. "Losing my little girl."

"That'll never happen." A tear managed to

escape the dam Cassidy tried to hold back. "So, don't you leave me."

"Aren't we a pair," he said. "I'm stressed because I fear losing you, which in turn, is stressing you because you want to be with me."

Cassidy laughed through her sobs.

"I'm sorry about what Karen and I did to you, Cass. We would never purposely hurt you."

"I know, Dad. Mom wasn't perfect, but we were blessed to have her. She was a wonderful mother to me. Somehow, I have to learn to forgive her." She smiled at Liam, hopeful. "You have to forgive her too, Dad."

He looked at Cassidy as if he was a misbehaved child, and she was his parent. "Do you forgive me?"

Cassidy brushed his hair from his face. He needed a haircut. Her father closed his eyes in bliss, from her gentle touch. "Yes, I forgive you, Dad. Now, so there are no more misunderstandings, I love you. Let's leave the past in the past."

A nurse walked into the room. She looked at his chart then took his vitals. "Ma'am, you, and your husband need to let him rest."

Liam grinned, holding his hand out to

Cassidy. "Wife," he said in jest. "Let's get something to eat, and let Dad rest."

"Lord, give me strength," she said, looking at the ceiling. She kissed her father's cheek again. "I'll be back in a few hours."

"Okay sweetheart." He gave her hand to Liam. "This is only temporary, but I'm willing to negotiate something permanent in the future."

Liam entwined his fingers with Cassidy's. "From your mouth to God's ears."

She swatted his arm. "Hey! Do I have a say so in the matter?"

Liam shook his head. "Nope. God's will be done, remember?"

Charles chuckled. "See you both in a few hours."

He looked more at peace than she'd seen him in years. "I love you, Dad. Try to get some sleep."

"I'm glad you're okay, Charles." Liam sighed heavily. "We need you to get well. I need an inflated ego when I beat you at chess. I also need you to referee when your daughter gets mad. Jeez, she has a temper!"

Cassidy playfully punched Liam in the stomach.

He dodged. "See what I mean?"

The nurse cleared her throat. "The patient."

"Yes, of course." Cassidy picked up her purse. "We're leaving."

Walking out of the room, Liam called over his shoulder, "We'll be back, Charles."

CHAPTER TWENTY-ONE

As they waited for the elevator, Cassidy stood on her tiptoes and kissed Liam fully on the lips.

"I'm not complaining, but what was that for?"

She gave him a Mona Lisa smile. "I've wanted to kiss you since the day you walked into my living room."

He looked at her questioningly. "I thought you weren't ready."

"I thought I wasn't either, but I am."

"What does the kiss mean? And, am I allowed to kiss you back?"

"Liam, you've been kind and patient. You've given us something tangible to build upon. I'm ready to give us a try—that is, if you still want to."

"Corinthians says love is patient and kind. It always protects, always trusts, always hopes, and always perseveres. Love never fails."

He leaned down and kissed her softly. Cassidy closed her eyes, then delayed before opening them. The kiss felt wonderful, a little bit of heaven on earth. Her heart burst with adoration.

"I'm so glad you came into our lives. I wish the circumstances were different. Pastor White says, 'God moves in mysterious ways.'"

"God brought all of us together because we needed each other." Liam grabbed both her hands and held them. "I want us to stay together because we love each other. I want us to be a family. For so long, I've desperately wanted to label someone as my family. The word is foreign to me, despite that, I'm eager to learn the language. You and Charles felt like family early in this relationship, but I was too close to the situation to be objective. That's why I stayed away those three weeks. I knew I wanted you two. I didn't know if you wanted me."

Cassidy rolled her eyes and gave him another endearing smile. "What? That's crazy!"

"No it's not. I was ecstatic when you called and invited me to dinner. Plus, I heard Charles in the background saying, 'Get over here Liam. I've missed you! I need a worthy adversary to play chess with.' I thought I'd have a heart attack. That phone call meant you guys wanted me too. Can you understand that?"

"You are nuts! We were dying inside. We hadn't had our Liam fix for three weeks."

He laughed. "Man, when I hung up the phone, I ran to the bathroom to shower, then I threw on some clothes and shoes. Believe it or not, I had a hard time buttoning my shirt! I broke all kinds of speed limits to get over to your house. It was time to unravel the mystery once and for all."

When the elevator doors opened, it was empty. They shared a grateful look for the alone time when they boarded.

Cassidy gave him a long impassioned stare. "You did all that just for my father's lasagna?"

In response, his eyes too blazed with passion. "I did all that to see how beautiful you looked when you opened the door. I did all that because I realized I wanted to be a part of your family."

"Silly Liam. You're already a part of our family." Cassidy's face held a teasing expression. The intoxicating chemistry between them always appeared thick and palpable. "If it's all the same with you, I don't want to be your little sister," she whispered in his ear.

His cheeks flushed. "Cassidy Fallows, you could never be my little sister. I'm aiming for a different familial title."

Cassidy laughed then caught him by the waist and held him. She felt his heart racing. "I want to try, just keep being patient with me."

Cautiously, Liam enclosed her in his arms, loosely at first, but when she didn't object, he tightened the grip. "I can do that."

She caressed the small of his back, encouraging his embrace. "If I'm totally honest Liam, what I feel for you scares me."

"This scares me too, Cassidy. I've been alone my whole life. Never committed to anyone. Yet and still, I want to give you and Charles everything I have inside me. I believe and trust in God. Our union is sacred because of Him."

Liam leaned in to kiss her again. The second kiss was more passionate and longer, and still just as intoxicating. Cassidy wondered if he was testing the waters to see if she gave him carte blanche.

No one had boarded the elevator, and they

were almost ground level. It was their first romantic interlude. Although the interlude was quick, the brief time was intense and intimate.

She placed her head on his chest, listening to the rapid beat of his heart. "Where do we go from here?"

His stomach growled. "To eat," he said with a grin. "I'm hungry."

After they walked out of the elevator, Liam picked up the arts section of the newspaper lying on a waiting room table. "Why, I'll be..." There was a picture of him and Cassidy on the front page. The caption read:

Cassidy Fallows is off the most eligible bachelorettes' list. Her new beau, Liam Papadakis, stood proudly by her side at her sold out art exhibit.

Cassidy laughed. "Well you know what they say," she said. "If it's written in the newspaper, it's got to be true."

"Amen to that." Liam winked at her. "Besides, I'm working on it."

They both laughed and walked out of the hospital, holding hands.

EPILOGUE

Guilt resonated throughout Cassidy's body. She shouldn't have waited over two years before visiting her mother's grave, no matter the circumstances. Holding white tulips, Cassidy stumbled through the cemetery, trying not to step on graves. Of all the flowers, she hated tulips, especially white ones. White tulips reminded her of her painful past.

That day would've been her mother's birthday, and white tulips were the only flowers her mother gave or received. In the spring, she would position the flowers all around their house. Ironically, white tulips symbolized forgiveness. Maybe her mother had been asking to be forgiven all along.

Cassidy bought a dozen flowers for her mother's transgressions and another dozen for hers. Karen had been a wonderful mother who showed her nothing but love. Forgiving her should've been an easy. Unfortunately, people aren't wired that way.

Forgiveness took Cassidy a lot longer.

That day, the sun shone brightly. Thank God, she wore shades to hide her tears, no one was the wiser. Her father and Liam stood a few feet away, waiting for her. She was late as Jax had kept her longer than she expected. He wanted her to be a partner, and mentor impoverished high school kids with a talent for painting. She jumped at the opportunity.

Liam grinned widely as she got closer to where he stood. After all this time, he still took her breath away. God had placed two great men in her life. She and Liam had been married a year.

He kissed Cassidy on the cheek. "Hey babe."

"Hey babe yourself," she said, eagerly accepting his kiss.

Liam had given Cassidy the affectionate moniker right after she conceded to his charms. She didn't mind it. He needed to say it, and sometimes when she felt down and out, she needed to hear it.

Her father kissed her forehead. "How's my little girl today?" He placed his hand on her stomach. "Hi little grandbaby," he said, in a cheerful voice.

"I'm fine Dad, just a little morning sickness. I'm in my second trimester now. The nausea should get better soon."

Liam grabbed her waist. "Are you ready to go visit Karen?"

She nodded then worriedly looked at her father. "Are you?"

He held out his arm to her. "Yes, I believe I am. This is an over-do visit. Karen deserved better."

Sandwich between the two men, Cassidy marched forth. "It's time. Let's go visit Mom." As they neared the grave, fresh white tulips were already there. When Cassidy glanced upward, she saw Peter walking away at a face pace. "Peter!"

Peter stopped and turned to face her. Cassidy gasped. His appearance was startling. Where he would normally look arrogant and cocky, he now looked meek and worn. His hair didn't have a hint of color in it. It was all gray. The whites of his eyes appeared cloudy.

"I saw you coming and…" he trailed off. "Anyway, I was just leaving."

Cassidy shook her head. "No, it's Mom's birthday. Everyone who loved her is entitled to be here." She looked at her father for approval.

He nodded. "Yes, Pete, you can stay."

Peter's eyes widened, surprised by the invitation. "Thank you." He looked at Liam.

"I'm sorry. I can't remember your name."

Liam held out his hand. "Liam Papadakis, Cassidy's husband."

This time, Peter gripped his hand firmly.

"Congratulations, I heard you were married." Peter looked at Cassidy. "Marriage suits you. You have a glow." His eyes widened again. "And looks like you have a new baby on the way."

Instinctively, she put her hand over her stomach. "I'm seventeen weeks."

Liam kissed her again. "There's never been a more beautiful expectant mother."

Cassidy knelt to place flowers on her mother's grave. "Hi Mom." She pulled a few weeds from around the heart shaped headstone. "A lot of things have happened since you left." She held up her hand. "I got married! Indirectly, you brought the most wonderful man into my life. And guess what else? You're going to be a grandmother," she whispered. "I promise to raise this baby in the way of the Lord, and with as much love as you raised me, which was an awful lot, Mom. Thank you for always showing me your love. Despite everything else, that's what I remember most about you—your love. This baby will know everything there is to know about Nana." She rose, kissed her fingers then touched Karen's headstone.

Liam put his roses down next. They represented love. He loved Cassidy and by proxy, he loved Karen. "I was angry with you, but from our family–yours and mine—I've learned who you were, and I'm quite impressed. I wish we could've met. You've raised a beautiful, smart and intelligent woman, and loved a brilliant and honorable man. Now, I feel blessed to have been on the dark road. I know Corky's with you. You two take care of each other."

When Charles put his flowers down, they were a mixture of white tulips and roses. They all walked away, giving him a private moment with his wife.

Peter stared at Cassidy. She became fidgety, biting her bottom lip, unable to find a comfortable stance. Liam placed his arm around her shoulder to comfort her.

Peter shifted his weight from one foot to the other. "You haven't had an exhibit in a while."

Cassidy gave a brittle smile. "I need inspiration to paint, which is something I haven't had a lot of lately." She grabbed Liam's waist and touched her stomach. "I feel my creativity coming back, though."

Her father joined them. His eyes were red and misty. "Are you two ready to go? We need to visit Corky too."

Cassidy shook her head. "I need to tell Mom something else." She knelt in front of the headstone again. "Mom, I apologize for waiting so long to visit. It won't happen again. I promise we will visit you frequently, and as a family, including Liam Jr."

Liam helped her up and wrapped his arms around her waist. "Liam Jr.?"

Her smile was mesmerizing, considerably beyond Liam's most beloved Mona Lisa smile. "Oh yeah, I had an ultrasound earlier today. We're having a boy!"

Liam picked her up and twirled her around. He'd told her he hoped to have a boy first. When he placed her feet back on solid ground, he kissed her. "God is good, isn't He?"

Cassidy gave him another kiss. Liam loved her and her father boundlessly, guiding their paths to God. Having his baby was the least she could do. "This baby isn't the reason I know of God's grace, honey. You are."

Charles slapped his son-in-law on the back and laughed. "A boy! That's wonderful news."

Peter started to walk away. "Congratulations everyone."

Her father caught his arm. He held on to it firmly. "It was good seeing you, Pete." He extended his hand, as if in remembrance of their childhood together.

Peter gently took his hand, possibly for the same reasons she suspected her father offered it. "It was good to see you too, Charlie." He glanced at Cassidy once more. "Your husband's right. I've never seen a more beautiful, pregnant woman."

"Thank you." She forced a smile. Forgiving Karen wasn't easy, yet she had. Peter's forgiveness would be even harder. Mustering strength of that magnitude would take years, if ever.

Peter must've felt her reticent mood. With his face dejected he turned to Liam. "Thank you for making her happy. I don't think I've ever seen her look more radiant, and alive."

Liam smiled widely, winking at Cassidy. "I'm working on it."

Cassidy, Liam and Charles walked away,

hugging each other. She looked behind them and Peter stood staring.

Lifting her head, she prayed.

Dear Lord, thank you for this day! You have blessed me so much. My cup runneth over. This prayer is not for me. This prayer is for Peter. Bless him Lord with peace, love and happiness. In Jesus name, I pray. Amen.

~THE END~

About the Author

Cheryl A. Daniels, Author

Cheryl decided that instead of reading another book, she'd write one. She wrote at every opportunity—at red lights, and stop signs; she even wrote in the middle of the night. Whenever the plot evolved in her mind, she'd write it down. Of course, she'd never written a book before in her life. Nor did she know the rules for writing. Driven to learn all she could about the topic, she enrolled in an online writing course that literally changed her life.

Mrs. Daniels lives in Texas with her husband and daughter. She adores her grandchildren and they visit her frequently. Cheryl is a proud mother, and cherishes a bond of friendship with her other three adult children.

Cheryl Daniels brings to Topaz Publishing, Inspirational and Christian Romance.

Email: cdlmo4@aol.com

Topazpublishingllc.com

Topazpublishing.webs.com

serendipityswomb.com